at Season's end

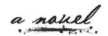

a novel

ERIC HENDERSHOT

SWEETWATER BOOKS

AN IMPRINT OF CEDAR FORT, INC.

SPRINGVILLE, UTAH

ISBN 13: 978-1-59955-995-7

Published by Sweetwater Books, an imprint of Cedar Fort, Inc.
2373 W. 700 S., Springville, UT 84663
Distributed by Cedar Fort, Inc., www.cedarfort.com

LIBRARY OF CONGRESS CATALOGING-IN-PUBLICATION DATA

Hendershot, Eric, author.
At season's end / Eric Hendershot.
pages cm
Summary: When Sal and her brother are suddenly orphaned during the Depression, the heartbroken teens load all their earthly possessions into the trunk of a travel-worn 1929 Buick and head out on the adventure of their lives.
ISBN 978-1-59955-995-7
1. Depressions--1929--Juvenile fiction. [1. Depressions--1929--Fiction. 2. Automobile travel--Fiction. 3. Orphans--Fiction. 4. Brothers and sisters--Fiction. 5. Family life--Fiction.] I. Title.

PZ7.H3786At 2012
[Fic]--dc23

2012001935

Cover design by Brian Halley
Cover design © 2012 by Lyle Mortimer
Edited and typeset by Kelley Konzak

Printed in the United States of America

10 9 8 7 6 5 4 3 2 1

Printed on acid-free paper

Praise for At Season's End

"*At Season's End* is funny and heartwarming. It made me want to quit my day job and live the adventurous life of a seasonal laborer."

—Jared Hess, writer/director of *Napolean Dynamite*, the movie and the hit animated series

"*At Season's End* is a charming and sweet tale that grabs the reader from beginning to end."

—Mike Fenton, Hollywood's "King of Casting" for movies such as the Back to the Future trilogy

"It's refreshing, uplifting and just plain fun reading. Just brilliant."

—Lee Benson, newspaper columnist and author of several books.

"This is a wonderful book; we enjoyed it immensely. Fascinating! *At Season's End* takes us to a place that all of us should know about: the life of a family of migrant workers in the '20s and '30s in the Northwest United States. Eric Hendershot is a master storyteller as he skillfully weaves the history and stalwart personalities of that era into our hearts and minds and reminds us that nothing is more important than having a strong family."

—Richard and Linda Eyre, speakers and authors of multiple books, including the *New York Times* #1 bestseller *Teaching Your Children Values*

"A wonderful and compelling love story! I could go on and on. I loved it! As I read I felt as is I was traveling right along with the family. Eric Hendershot is a wonderful storyteller."

—Merrill Jensen, Emmy Award–winning composer

"I loved, loved, loved *At Season's End*! It is a heartwarming and amazing book! Readers won't know what hit them."

—Melissa Magleby, dancer for Odyssey Dance Theatre

"*At Season's End* has amazing characters that literally pull you into this heartwarming love story!"

—Greg Porter, founder and CEO of Powerschool

"I was delighted with it!

"This is a heartwarming story, one that draws the reader in quickly. It was delightful to journey with the fruit pickers, and then the two young children set adrift. It was interesting to find yourself cheering for a young marriage that normally, you would be counseling against! A great reminder of the meaningfulness of the lives of ordinary people! This is a book for readers of all ages."

—Becky Douglas, founder and president
of Rising Star Outreach

"Eric Hendershot has crafted a highly entertaining period novel, laced with heart and humor that will bring you hope and insight into the human condition. I highly recommend it!"

—TC Christensen, writer/director of *17 Miracles*

"Eric Hendershot's creation of period and place and use of migrant dialogue invites the reader on an authentic journey into the past . . . remembering people from an almost forgotten era."

—Keith Merrill, Academy Award winner and author
of *The Evolution of Thomas Hall*

Author's Note

THIS BOOK IS DEDICATED TO MRS. REBA LAZENBY (1914–2006), because without Reba, there would be no book.

Reba first met the character Tim in 1961. He worked for a local feed mill and lived in a small shack across the road from Reba and her family. One day, the feed mill owner brought Tim to Reba's door and asked Reba if Tim could have access to the water tap in her front yard because the shack Tim was living in had no water. Reba readily agreed.

One evening, Reba invited Tim over for supper, and after that, he came over quite often. During these times, Tim would tell Reba and her family about some of his experiences traveling across the country following crops. Reba recalls Tim saying after they watched TV one night, "I could write a story that would put all them TV plays to shame."

"Why don't you?" Reba asked.

"If I wrote it, would you read it?" Tim asked excitedly. Reba assured him that she would.

That very night, Tim started to write in longhand at the little kitchen table in the shack.

He would finish three or four pages a night and bring

them over. Reba and her family read them and could hardly wait for the next night to find out what would happen next. Tim didn't tell them it was the story of his life until Reba asked him. Then he admitted that it was all true and that he was the Tim in the story.

One day, Tim's boss asked him to take one of the big trucks to a neighboring town to pick up a load of grain. Tim did not want to go, but the boss insisted. As Tim neared the town, he drove into a roadblock that was set up to check driver's licenses. He was ticketed for driving without a license. He left that night and was never seen again by Reba and her family. The ticket was left on the table in the shack.

Years later, Reba became friends with my wife's father, Richard Dorius Johnson (1912–2008). Richard was deeply moved by the story and encouraged me to write a screenplay, which I agreed to do.

As I re-edited and pieced the story together chronologically, I began questioning if Tim's story was really true. I decided to do a little detective work. In the story, Tim's family has an unusual experience at Big Mama's Truck Stop in Goodwater, Alabama. *Was there really a Big Mama's Truck Stop?* I wondered. I called information and got the number for Goodwater's Chamber of Commerce. The lady I spoke with said she had never heard of the place. Then she said, "Hold on a minute. Let me give you the number of the oldest man in Goodwater. If anyone would remember this place, he would." After a moment, she came back to the phone and gave me the number. I called the old gentleman, introduced myself, and asked, "Do you by chance remember Big Mama's Truck Stop?" He thought for a moment, then said, "Yes, there was a place called Big Mama's Truck Stop. It was on the edge of town."

I can't tell you how excited I was. After months of writing and researching, I had the opportunity to go to Hood River, Oregon, where much of this story takes place. As I walked through a cherry orchard there and thought of Tim and his family and the arduous road they traveled, I was moved to tears.

I believe as you read this heartrending, soul-stirring story of love, you will experience a wide range of emotions like I did. You will laugh and cry and, above all, redefine your definition of what a hero really is.

Eric Hendershot

One

FORTY BOB

MILE AFTER MILE PAW HAD BEEN DRIVIN' SEEMED LIKE HE would never stop. 'Taint like Paw to do that. Most of the time he would stop to give Tim and me a chance to stretch our legs.

We're late this year, after spendin' the winter in Florida pickin' citrus. Trouble is, an early frost killed most of the fruit. We never made hardly enough to live on, and sure not enough to meet travelin' expenses.

Before we got out of Louisiana we were broke, and since then, we'd stop along the way to find work. Like one place where Paw got a job cleanin' hen houses, and we all pitched in to help; and another place where we built a fence for a farmer—just anythin' and everythin' we could find to earn a little to go on. Like always, we wanted to get into Idaho to train hops, but already we knew we were too late. So we changed directions and started west for Washington, goin' north and then across Montana.

Now we're in northern Montana on Highway US 2, just goin' through south Glacier National Park. Through the car windows, I see and feel the beauty of this country, with mountains and tall pine trees reachin' nearly to the sky, so it seems, gently wavin' in the fadin' light.

The trouble is, we're broke again and have only a little over half a tank of gas in this old, overloaded Buick. Besides that, I'm hungry—really hungry—only there ain't no use in sayin' nothin' 'cause I know we're all hungry.

Tim, my little brother one year younger than me, is twelve now and looks and acts so much like Paw—the same steady gray eyes and mouse brown hair; the same slight frame. He even talks low and easy like Paw, never raisin' his voice for nothin'.

Out of the clear blue, Paw started singin', and Maw joined in: "Oh, we ain't got a barrel o' money, mebby we're ragged and funny, but we travel along, singin' a song, side by side."

Paw could sing with the best of them, but Maw couldn't carry a tune in a bucket if she wanted. But it didn't matter. I always loved to hear them sing together. Then Tim and me joined in for the rest of it: "Don't know what's comin' tomorrow, mebby it's trouble and sorrow, but we travel the road, sharin' our load, side by side."

Suddenly, as we came around the next curve deep in the mountain, Paw slammed on the brakes and brought the big Buick to a screechin' halt just in front of a little foreign-made car. Then, backin' up to it, he asks, "Trouble, stranger?" A short, fat fellow, wearin' suspenders, had the hood up and was starin' down at the engine like it was the first time he'd ever seen one.

"Don't know," said the stranger, wipin' perspiration from the top of his shiny bald head. Then he looked over at Paw and said, "Would you be kind enough to stop at the next town and send a man out?"

"Too far," said Paw as he got out of the car, grabbed

a chain from under his feet, and hooked it to the bumper of the little car.

"Hold on a minute!" said the stranger. "What you fixin' to do?"

Only Paw didn't hold on; he just hooked the cars together, then said, "'Tis 'most forty miles to the next town, and they could charge a heap to come way out here."

By that time, Paw was back in the Buick, engagin' the clutch. Without sayin' no more, he started up real easy. The poor man couldn't help himself; all he could do was jump in his car before Paw pulled away. Besides, he had a girl with him 'bout my age, and I suppose he didn't want to lose her.

Mebby I should state here that Paw would stop and help anyone, even if they didn't have a nickel, but I know this time Paw is hopin' to get a couple o' "bobs" to eat on.

Tim said, "Paw, I bet that feller thinks we're crazy, the way we're loaded and all."

Maw just laughed. But it was true. We was a wondrous sight to behold. Most of what we owned was piled on the car. We had bed springs on the top, a small iron cook stove on the runnin' board, and a battered trunk and a galvanized wash tub tied on behind.

I turned around in my seat and looked at the stranger out the back window. He was yellin', but we couldn't hear a thing he was sayin'. But I could read his lips. He was shoutin', "SLOW DOWN! SLOW DOWN!" I didn't blame him 'cause Paw was drivin' 'bout forty around those crooked mountain roads, slowin' down only when the curve was too sharp. Every time we went around a curve, we could hear the tires screechin'.

Bein' tired of settin', and gettin' restless, Tim started

snappin' Paw's ear with his finger, swearin' 'twas a bug. The rest of the way, we played back and forth with Paw and Maw, with the stranger bein' towed behind.

Sure enough, it was 'most forty miles before Paw stopped in town, next to a garage and restaurant together. As we got out, the stranger came up and said, "Boy, you are quite a driver, what with those children on you like monkeys, goin' 'round those curves! At first I just knew we were goin' to fall 'bout a hundred feet. Why, when I saw them carryin' on, I just knew we'd all die. I started prayin' for my sins, your sins, and 'bout everyone I know and some I don't." And he laughed a hearty laugh. "What do I owe you?" he asked.

"Owe us?" said Paw like his feelings were hurt. "Why, you don't owe us nothin'."

For a minute, I thought Paw had flipped. I knew we are all hungry, and Paw says the man don't owe nothin'. To Tim I whispered, "Why is Paw turnin' down a bob that way?"

Tim looked at me with his eyes laughin'. "Don't you worry none," he said, "Paw knows what he's about. I suppose he's turned down a bob—so's he can get two."

"What?" said the stranger. "You haul me all that way, and I don't owe you nothin'?"

"Well," Paw said, "the Lord has been good to us. Mebby He took all our worldly possessions, but He spared all our lives."

"Come, now," said the stranger, takin' Paw by the arm, "at least come in with me and have a cup of coffee; 'tis the least I could do."

Rubbin' his chin, Paw said, "Well, if you insist, but we ain't a-lookin' for nothin'."

Then Paw said, "Meet the wife, and this is Tim," he added, puttin' his hand on Tim's head. "Sally, there, we just call her Sal, and I'm Paw to 'most everyone."

"Erven, Erven Goody," said the stranger, puttin' out his hand, "and this here is my daughter, Rozella." She was a small girl, with red hair and a face full of freckles and the deepest blue eyes I had ever seen.

Once inside the restaurant, we all sat at a long table, Maw and Paw each sittin' at the end of the table, Erven next to Paw on his right, Rozella at her dad's right, while I sat to the right of Maw, and Tim next to me on my right.

While we were waitin' for service, Mr. Goody started askin' questions, like where we're from, where we're goin', and how come. Of course, it is to be remembered that he asked one question at a time, and Paw answered one at a time. This is what Paw told him:

"Well," Paw drawled, "Our home burned down in Florida, and we're on our way to my brother's in Oregon."

Of course none of this was true. But Paw told it so good, with his voice soundin' so true and honest that I believed it myself.

"Sure sorry to hear that," said Mr. Goody. "I mean, your home burnin'."

"Really, we don't mind so much," Paw said. "God spared our lives, and we're all together. There ain't nothin' more important than family."

"I couldn't agree with you more," said Mr. Goody, puttin' his arm around Rozella and givin' her an affection-ate squeeze. "I sure hope you had insurance."

"Well, did have at one time," said Paw sadly, "but been out of work so long we finally had to drop it."

"Too bad! Too bad!" said Mr. Goody, shakin' his

head, and I could see he was really sorry.

By that time our food was bein' served, a very nice dinner with fried chicken and all the trimmings.

You should know that we did have a house once. It didn't burn down like Paw was tellin' Mr. Goody, but it might as well have 'cause we had to give it back to the bank who owned it. It was all on account of what they called the Great Depression of 1929. Like a thick black cloud, that depression hunkered down so hard on the country that lots of good, hardworkin' folks just like us lost everythin' it took a lifetime to gather. Money got real scarce, and crop prices dropped some sixty percent. Hard as they tried, Paw and Maw couldn't hang on any longer. Up until then, Paw farmed our ten acres, and when he wasn't farmin', he did all kinds of odd jobs like drillin' wells, mendin' fences, overhaulin' tractors, or buildin' barns and outbuildings for other farmers. Wasn't much Paw couldn't fix, and if there wasn't a tool to fix it, Paw would make one. But when nobody's got no money, they can't afford to have all those things done.

Lots of folks blamed that joyless time on the stock market crash. It supposedly all came about on a Tuesday, October 29, 1929. That day was forever called "Black Tuesday." That was the right name for it all right, 'cause there never was or has been since a time so bleak, dark, and hopeless as that awful season was. Paw didn't blame the Depression on the crash. He blamed the government. I can still hear him say, and when he was sayin' it he was always spittin' mad, 'Why in tarnation are they raisin' taxes when unemployment's at twenty-five percent? If they would just get out of our dang way and quit tryin' to regulate everythin', things would fix their selves!" I didn't know much 'bout what was goin' on, but I figured Paw was probably right, 'cause after all, he was the smartest man I knew. Yes—those were painful times. In 1931, the Empire State Buildin' was bein' built at the whoppin' cost of forty million dollars, while in its shadow starvin' men fought over piles of garbage to feed their families.

I will never forget that day long as I live when Paw and Maw called me and Tim out to the porch to talk to us. I have never seen either of them look so downright serious. Both of them had tears wellin' up their eyes.

"Young'uns," said Paw, "we've got some bad news."

At first I thought for sure Paw was gonna tell us that he or Maw was dyin'. When he told us there was gonna be a sheriff's sale and that we were gonna lose the farm, I burst into tears and threw my arms around Paw's neck.

"It's okay, little darlin'," said Paw, "don't you worry. We'll find us another place by and by, just soon as things get better."

"Oh, Paw!" I cried, "I don't care a hoot about the farm! The way you and Maw were actin', I thought for sure one of you was dying! I'm not cryin' 'cause I'm sad. I'm cryin' 'cause I'm so happy that you and Maw are okay." Then I hugged him again. Then Paw and Maw shared a look that, as long as I live, I will never forget. I saw hope and determination light up their eyes like I had never seen before. Yes, things were tougher than they had ever been, but they still had each other and they had family, and there was nothin' more important.

A couple of days later, Paw left to find work. I can tell you we all missed him terrible. I can still hear Maw cryin' herself to sleep at night.

One day, 'bout a week later, right around supper time

while me and Tim were helpin' Maw get dinner, we heard the screen door behind us open and bang shut. When we turned to look, there was Paw standin' in the doorway. He was smilin' real big, with his arms reachin' out for us. We all shouted, "Paw!" and ran to him. As he held us all in his arms, he told us right there that he missed us too much and had a plan that would keep us together as a family.

It was a cruel fact that many men durin' those tough times abandoned their families and forced their wives and children to fend for their selves. I say shame on them. If only they had stuck it out like our Paw, they would have learned that good can come from bad and meanin' can come from tragedy.

A couple of days later, with the old Buick packed chock-full and only two dollars in Paw's pocket, we drove away from the farm lookin' for work.

We drove all the way to New York with Paw doin' whatever he had to do to keep gas in the car and food in our bellies. In New York, we got work pickin' berries, gettin' paid a cent and a half a quart and eight baskets for twelve cents. We worked ten hours and made two dollars and forty-four cents. That may not seem like much, but at that time, a quarter could feed a man for a whole day.

Anyhow, that was more than two years ago. Since then we've seen just about every inch of this great country and done just 'bout everythin' to keep ourselves a-gettin' and a-goin'.

Now here we are somewhere in Montana, flat busted broke and wonderin' where our next bob's gonna come from. But I ain't worried much 'cause so far the good Lord's been watchin' out for us and got us where we are. And besides the good Lord, we got Paw.

Anyhow, after we ate our chicken dinner, Mr. Goody ordered for dessert a whole lemon meringue pie. Maw cut everyone a slice, and we all dug in. I have never tasted in my whole life anythin' more delicious. When we finished up the pie, Paw laid down his napkin and said, "Well, I guess we better be a-gettin' and a-goin'."

"Now hold on," said Mr. Goody, reachin' for his billfold. "Before you go, I'd like to pay you for your help today."

"Pay us?" said Paw like he was shocked that Mr. Goody would even dare to declare such a thing. "Why, we just had the best dinner we've had since I can't remember. No sir, you've already been more than generous."

What is Paw doin' turnin' down help? I thought to myself. I looked at Tim tryin' to hide the panic I was feelin' inside. But Tim just looked back at me with a wink and a half smile. That was his way of tellin' me to quit bein' so carked and watch how Paw was gonna get what he needed. I hoped against hope that Tim was right.

"With all your troubles," said Mr. Goody, "you stopped for us and won't let us pay you for your trouble?" Mr. Goody asked.

Paw began rubbin' his chin and said, "Well, it's this way. When the good Lord helped someone, and He helped many, can't recall Him ever chargin'. I believe we should help one another without lookin' for some pay. Nope. God will look after us. You see, God had already supplied us with our first meal today, and I suppose He'll help us find a job to earn enough to get us to where we're goin'."

"You mean you're broke?" said Mr. Goody.

"Don't you worry none 'bout us. God will care for His. No sir, God won't turn His back on us."

There was silence for a spell, then Mr. Goody said, "Look here, I know you're good, God-fearin' people. I can always tell a man by what his children are, and yours are good mannered and polite. Yes, you're a good family, and I know you won't take pay for what you did, but let me make you a loan."

Tim looked at me as if to say, "What did I tell you?"

Again rubbin' his chin, Paw answered, "Well, I don't know. 'Twill cost a heap yet, 'most forty dollars, to get us there. And you don't even know us."

"I know enough," said Mr. Goody, passin' Paw a card. "Here's my name and address."

Takin' the card, Paw passed it to Maw.

"And here's forty dollars," said Mr. Goody, takin' a twenty and two tens from his billfold. This Paw put in his pocket.

"There should be more in the world like you," said Mr. Goody, "so willin' to help."

After Paw and the stranger got through tellin' each other how good each other were, we was soon on our way again. As we drove off, Maw dropped Mr. Goody's business card out the window.

You may think that wasn't right—Maw droppin' Mr. Goody's card like she did—but chances of us ever havin' an extra forty dollars would be few and far between. And if by chance we ever did have extra, Paw would make sure someone 'sides us would surely get it, as you will soon learn.

Two

HOOD RIVER CAMP

AFTER WE LEFT MONTANA, WE DROVE ACROSS NORTHERN Idaho, into Washington, then south into the small town of Hood River, Oregon. Before we got to town, we stopped near the river to wash, cook, and clean up. Our camp was on the great Columbia River, that swift, treacherous river that has claimed many lives. While Tim gathered wood for a fire, Paw unloaded the car of the things we would need and Maw and I peeled taters for supper, 'cause all must do their share of work—never dependin' on someone else to do it all. Then, like Maw said, "Tomorrow, we'll all be rested and cleaned up—time enough then to find a job."

After supper was cleared, by the light of the fire, Paw read to us from the Bible, like it was his habit. Then we all took turns thankin' God for the blessings that we had received.

"'Tain't right," Paw said thoughtfully, "to tell whoppers like I did back yonder, but we gotta get by somehow. If I told that feller he owed me ten dollars, mebby he would think I overcharged him and tell me I had no business hookin' him to us like I did. No, 'tain't right. But

I guess it is a necessary evil—for us, at least. Nope, 'tain't right, though. May God forgive me."

After worship, while the fire was low, Maw and Paw sat side by side, leanin' against a great pine tree. Tim was leanin' against Paw, and I laid my head in Maw's lap. Lookin' up at her, I just knew she was the most beautiful woman in the world. Her deep brown eyes, with the most gentle expression I've ever seen, glowed softly in the moonlight.

My hair was to my shoulders. My eyes are brown like hers, and I also have an oval face, but that is where our resemblance ends. Where she had well-rounded arms and legs, mine were skinny and seemed to me they were too long. Where Maw had the curves in the right places, I was like a beanpole. Laughin', Paw had told me not to worry, that I was like a young filly, and by and by I'd fill out too.

The only sounds were the crickets, accompanied by the deeper sounds of bullfrogs, till Maw and Paw started singin' "Home, Sweet Home." Only they didn't sing loud; they were singin' it real low, like the breeze through the pine boughs. Closin' my eyes, I could see home as a campground with acres of green grass to run through, a stream runnin' by, and our washin' hangin' to dry on a limb close by. That was the only real home we had known for the past three years. Be it ever so humble, there's no place like home.

About nine the next mornin', we were up and ready to go look for a job. "Come on, young'uns, time to be a-gettin' and a-goin'," said Paw. We was in the car, ready to go, when Paw, all of a sudden, threw his door open, jumped out of the car, and started runnin' toward the river fast as he could.

"What is it, Paw? What's the matter?" shouted Maw. Then she jumped out the other side and ran after Paw.

Tim jumped out and started after them. "Wait fer me! Hey, wait up!" he yelled.

Now, I wasn't goin' to be the only one left behind. As I got out, I yelled, "Have you all gone crazy?"

There was Paw in the lead, goin' as hard as he could, then Maw, Tim next, and me tryin' to catch up, knowin' they must all be crazy. Even the river didn't stop Paw. Clothes and all, he jumped into the whirlin', swirlin' waters of the great Columbia.

At this, Maw let out a scream. Mebby she thought Paw was goin' to end it all. Then Tim yelled, "Oh, no, Paw!" But I was too surprised and scared to say anythin'.

I suppose it was just a second or two, but it seemed like minutes before he came up again to show us he had two heads and four arms. Then the mighty water turned him over to prove he had four legs. That was when we realized Paw was holdin' on for dear life to a young, drownin' boy.

Maw started runnin' down along the edge of the river-bank, chasin' after Paw and the boy. "This way, Paw, this way!" she kept on shoutin'.

"You can make it, Paw," Tim cried. "You can make it!"

"Dear God," I prayed, "he's just *gotta* make it!"

There wasn't much we could do—'cept just run along that bank, keepin' up with Paw and the boy he was tryin' to save. Seemed that sometimes he would almost reach shore, just to be flung away again like a leaf, back into the swirlin' deep.

Now, Paw was only five feet, five and a half inches tall and only weighed about 125 pounds, and we could see the water was gettin' the best of him. Sometimes they would go clear under, and sometimes their heads would be up and we could see that boy kickin' and strugglin' like a young demon.

Still Maw kept callin', "This way, honey, this way!" while Tim kept callin', "You can do it, Paw, you can do it! You know you can."

Finally the powerful current swept him closer to us. Maw was movin' now—faster'n I'd ever seen a body move—downstream along the riverbank. Pointin' at a nearby poplar tree, she yelled to Tim to get a good long limb. Tim did as he was told and soon caught up to Maw.

In seconds, Maw took the limb and ran out into the water to her waist, just ahead of Paw and the boy, and shoved that limb into the river just as Paw and the boy got there.

"Grab it, darlin'! Grab it!" she shouted.

Two of the four hands got a good grip on that limb, and Maw motioned for me and Tim to grab the end of it. "Grab it!" she shouted.

And we did—and pulled with all our might. I guess the three of us pullin' was better than that ol' river, 'cause Paw and the boy was closer to shore now. Maw got down on her belly, reached out, and grabbed the only thing she could, a handful of Paw's hair, and gave it a tremendous yank. As Paw got closer, both Tim and I grabbed a handful of hair and pulled him to shore, while he still held onto that strugglin' demon.

When we finally got them to shore, Maw threw herself across Paw's body and cradled his head in her arms. She was sobbin' with relief that Paw was still alive and breathin'. She held him tight and kept sayin' "I love you, Paw. I love you."

And there I was, on my hands and knees starin' down into the handsomest face I'd ever seen. I quickly stood, walked to a big rock, and sat down.

Both Paw and the boy were plum tuckered out and laid like they was near dead, with their eyes closed. Maw took their clothes off and hung them up to dry, leavin' only their shorts on. Both of them were takin' great breaths of air like there wasn't enough to go 'round.

For a good half hour they laid there. Finally Paw opened his eyes and said, "Shoot, dad gum, I thought if the river didn't get us, a bunch of Indians were goin' to snatch me ball-headed."

Maw was sittin' on the ground by Paw; Tim was kneelin' by the boy; and I was still sittin' on the big rock behind him. "Live hereabouts?" asked Paw of the boy. And I could see he was about my age or mebby a little older, with curly dark hair and brown eyes.

"In a shelter up the line," the boy answered.

"Yer name?" Paw asked.

"Ben Musgrove," he answered. "We just got here. Hope to start pickin' cherries soon."

"Yer paw got a job?" Paw asked the boy.

"Sure, but won't start work for a few days," the boy said.

"Yer boss need more help?" Paw inquired.

"'Spect so. He has more empty shelters," the boy answered.

For a while all was silent. Then Paw got up, started to dress, thought better of it, and told Tim to go fetch him some dry clothes.

Ben got up, and when he turned around, he saw me and looked at himself. "Gosh, girls!" he yelped, runnin' behind some bushes. Paw laughed and tossed him his clothes.

After Paw and Ben were dressed, Maw asked, "What were you doin' in there?"

"Fishin'," Ben said.

"Fishin'?" she repeated in surprise.

"Yep," Ben said and then continued, "Paw told me I could fish in that stream that enters this river. I lost my pole and, when I tried to get it, slipped and fell in. I tried to swim back, but the river had other ideas. What's yer name?" asked Ben.

"Oh," Paw drawled, "all my friends just call me Paw, and she's Maw to most folks. That's Sal there, and Tim."

Ben smiled and nodded and then said, "Pleased to meet ya."

When he smiled, seemed like my silly heart did a flip flop. I couldn't remember when I had seen such a handsome boy as this.

"Boy, just wait till I tell my paw what you did fer me!" said Ben.

"Oh, no, you don't," said Paw firmly.

"But I gotta tell him," Ben said, puzzled.

"You do," Paw mused, scoldin' a bit and lookin' like he meant it, "and I'll throw you in where I got you. Nope, boy, don't you dare tell anyone, not nary a soul. I ain't havin' no one pattin' me on the back. You just keep your mouth shut. Now, you promise, or I'll throw you back in that abominable river right now."

"Well, gee, gosh, all right. I won't tell no one," Ben said reluctantly, "but you saved my life, and I think they should know. How'm I goin' to explain these wet clothes if I don't tell them you risked your life fer me?"

"I don't care what you tell them. Tell them God helped you. Tell them unseen hands pulled you out. But don't you dare tell them 'twas me," said Paw, still as firm as before. Then Paw looked Ben square in the eyes and said, "Mebby someday you can do somethin' for me."

Now I know Paw didn't mean nothin' by this. He was just talkin' and never woulda guessed in a million years that one day his words would come true. It was no accident that Paw looked out that window when he did and saw Ben bobbin' up and down in that terrible river, 'bout ready to be drowned. In just a bit, we woulda been a-gettin' and a-goin' on our way, and Ben would, as sure as the night follows the day, have perished and vanished under those awful frightenin' waves. What made Paw look just when he did? Was it someone or somethin' that tapped him on the shoulder or mebby whispered in his ear and told him to look when he did? I never thought to ask him. I didn't have to 'cause I knew it wasn't no accident. Someone that could see into the future and knew what the years would bring told Paw to look.

Paw's eyes were still fixed on Ben. "Until then don't you tell nary a soul."

"Oh, all right," Ben said, "I promise. But, mister, I'll never forget what you done."

Ben rode with us to within a quarter mile from the shelters and told us to go straight ahead to the end of the road to find their boss.

The boss was a tall Swede by the name of Johnson. Sure, he needed more help, but it would be a couple of days, mebby four, before he could use us.

"How many of you are workin'?" he asked.

"All of us," Paw replied matter-of-fact.

He looked us all over careful like, and I knew what he was thinkin'. Maw and Paw was gettin' older. They didn't get married until later in their lives. Maw always called us kids her miracles 'cause she was in her forties when she finally had us. The hard work and bein' in the sun most all the time was takin' its effect on both of them, but mostly on Maw. Just in the last year, Paw's hair had gone completely white, and Maw's was beginnin' to get that way too.

Paw knew what Mr. Johnson was thinkin' and soon spoke up. "We may not look like much, but we'll work the big ladders and outpick anybody here."

I could tell Mr. Johnson liked Paw's pluck 'cause he nodded his head and broke into a smile. Then lookin' me and Tim over, he said, "They're pretty young."

"Yer not hirin' them," Paw said, "yer hirin' me, payin' by the pound. What we do to get those boxes full is our business."

Laughin', Mr. Johnson said, "Okay, you'll do. Go back to the shelters and take your pick of what's empty. We'll see you in a couple of days."

As we drove to the shelters, we were some surprised. It was a much better place than some we had been in. That is, there were large pine trees around the edge of the clearin' nestled in the bottom of the mountains, with a stream runnin' along one side. Five cabins or shelters were sittin' next to the stream, and on the other side of the clearin' was another set of six cabins. Close to the center of the clearin' was four more. Drivin' slowly, Paw looked the camp over. Then, drivin' next to the creek, he stopped under a large pine.

Out of the nearest cabin came a man and a woman.

The fellow was mebby five foot ten or eleven inches tall, a well-built, jolly-lookin' sort of man with dark hair, while his wife was a tiny thing, very pleasant lookin'. As they came out, they said, "Howdy, strangers."

"Howdy," we answered.

Comin' to the car and puttin' out his hand for Paw, the man said, "Musgrove's the name. This here is my wife Clara. My first name's Frank."

After all the introductions were made, Paw asked, "Any empties 'long here? And where is everybody? Don't see no cars, 'cept yours."

Mr. Musgrove began pointin' at the different shelters. "Course, we got this shelter. The Sawyers have that one just to the other side of me. They've gone to town. Mighty nice people; think you'll like them. Those other three are empty. If you don't like them, you'll find a couple empty in the center there."

"This'll do fine," Paw said, takin' the one next to Musgrove's, leavin' one empty on the end, next to us.

Three

NEW FRIENDS

THAT NIGHT WE ALL SAT UNDER THE BIG PINE TREE IN FRONT of the Musgroves' shelter. Clara brought out coffee and cups for all of us. Then Ben came from across the clearin' and sat down by the fire. When I looked at him, a peculiar thing happened. My heart began to flitter and I could feel my face goin' from warm to hot. I was grateful that it was dark and no one could see me flushin' the way I was.

Ben looked different. He wasn't bone weary from fightin' them terrible waves. His hair was dry, thick, and all blanched from the sun. He was barefoot, wearin' a pair of worn-out overalls over a collared shirt that was missin' some buttons here and there. I can say as one who had traveled most of this great country that Ben was the grandest and handsomest boy I had ever seen.

Frank asked, "Did you notice that creek 'long the highway before you came back on this road?"

"Yeah, we noticed it. Looks like some good fishin'," Paw said soberly.

"My boy Ben here," Frank said, pointin' at Ben, "was fishin'. Come home all wet. Says he fell in. Can't see how such a youngster ever got out of that ragin' current, and he can't make it none too clear, either—says somethin' 'bout God gettin' him out. Then says somethin' 'bout unseen hands. We can't make heads nor tails of it."

"Well," Paw drawled, tippin' his head back like he's in deep thought and rubbin' his chin, "mebby God did help. Mebby—just mebby a brush hangin' over the side rubbin' him would seem like unseen hands to him. Then again, mebby God just gave him a hand."

"I suppose you're right. But, mind you," Frank said, turnin' to Ben, "you stay away from that stream. You're the only young'un I got."

"Yes, Paw. I'll stay clear," said Ben.

Lookin' at him all cleaned up the way he was with that natural wavy hair all combed and all, and those laughin' brown eyes, my heart went out to him.

"Wanna look around?" Ben asked Tim as he finished his coffee.

"Sure do, but better I help unload first," Tim replied.

"I'll help," Ben said, "if yer paw says okay."

Our car was packed like any other migrant's car. On the floorboard between the front and back seats was our ironin' board, broom, and mop. On top of that was some old blankets, then our work clothes, then more blankets and pillows till it was level across from the top of the front seat to the top of the backseat. The back window had an old radio, an old clock, Tim's old truck about six inches long with both hind wheels missin', and my old doll with one arm and all the hair long gone.

In front, between Maw and Paw, was a thermos bottle and four cups, and under Maw's feet was a box that, if we were lucky, had crackers or bread or somethin' else to chew on.

The trunk had an old tub full of dishes and a kettle, and mebby, if we were lucky, a box of groceries, an old tire and what tools we had, and a suitcase with our good clothes in it.

It didn't take long to unload, as all the Musgroves gave us a hand. Then, as Tim and Ben started away, I just stood lookin' till Ben looked back at me and said, "You can come if you wanna."

I could feel myself flutter but didn't let it show. Course I wanted to go. Bein' on the road most of the time, I hardly ever got to meet anybody—'specially boys my age. Ben stood there waitin' for my answer. I tried to hide the excitement that was churnin' inside of me and, with a straight face, looked at Maw, hopin' against hope that she didn't need me to help her get the cabin settled.

When my eyes met Maw's, she could tell at once that I was anythin' but casual. She could read it in my eyes just how badly I wanted to be included. Maw seemed to have a secret sense to know what I was always thinkin'. I quit tryin' to lie to her long ago 'cause I never could get away with it. It was either a sense she had or mebby it was just the way God made mothers so they could watch out for His children until they came home again to Him. With a twinkle in her eye and a knowin' smile, she sent me on my way.

'Bout two hundred yards or so from camp was a big clearin', edged by tall pines that seemed to reach clear to the sky. And right through it ran a stream that emptied into the great Columbia. It was the most quietest and peaceful place I think I have ever been to. When we got to the pines, Tim ran off, leavin' me and Ben by ourselves. We sat down on a soft bed of pine needles under one of the giant pines and just talked. This was the very first time that I had ever been alone with a boy just talkin'. Any other time I woulda been cowed, but with Ben it felt so easy and natural. We talked and laughed till our folks finally called us to bed.

I learned that Ben was from Florida and that he and his maw and paw worked pickin' citrus. But soon they had to get on the road, like us, to find work elsewhere 'cause the crops got damaged by the great hurricanes of '26 and then '28. And if that wasn't bad enough, that terrible fruit fly of '29 ate up 'bout half of all the crops that was left. So just like us, they packed up and went searchin' for work. Ben told me they had just come from Kern County, California, where they helped with the potato harvest. That was how come half their trunk was filled with taters. Many times after the harvest, the farmers would let the migrants go through the fields and help themselves to what little if anythin' was left. It was called "gleanin'." I know that's what it's called 'cause Paw read to us from the Bible, in the book of Ruth, many times how Ruth had gathered or gleaned the leftover grain in the field of a man named Boaz.

Ben said that when he got old enough, he wanted to get his own farm and settle and work it like respectable folks. He said he was gettin' real tired of all the travelin' all over tarnation in the backseat of his parent's car. He said he wanted to make a home for his folks before they got too old to work.

I wasn't sure I agreed with everythin' he was sayin'. Course, I didn't say so. Truth was, I loved travelin' and seein' new places and meetin' new people. Mebby, like Ben, I too would get tired of it. And it was true Maw and Paw was gettin' older. What would we do when they got too old to work? For now I wasn't gonna worry none. Right then I was just happy to be here with a roof over my head, food to eat, and cherries to pick.

THE GRIFFINS

WHEN WE RETURNED FROM THE PINES, THE SAWYER FAMILY, the Musgroves, and our folks were still sittin' under the pine tree enjoyin' each other's company and gettin' better acquainted. It was then that we seen a car with headlights approachin'. The license plates said the car was all the way from West Virgina. But shucks, you can't go by that. Our plates showed Oklahoma; the Sawyers' showed Texas; and the Musgroves' showed Missouri. You could tell by the way the car was loaded that they weren't migrants. They knew nothin' 'bout packin'.

Four or five dogs ran to the car, sniffed around, then went back to their owners. A tall man got out from under the wheel. He was real thin, like mebby 'twas just bones with a little skin drawn over. Then the lady got out. She was just the opposite—real short and heavy, much too heavy for climbin' ladders all day. The back door opened, and out fell a bunch of clothes that had been piled against the door. Five kids got out: three girls and two boys, from 'bout thirteen to mebby eighteen. This is just guessin'. They were all tall and on the lean side like their paw.

Course we all said, "Howdy," to be polite.

"Howdy," said the man. "The boss said someone here would show us a house to live in."

Paw spoke up in an exaggerated drawl, "Shore will. Now there's an empty one right there," he said, pointin' to the shelter right next to ours.

"A house!" cried the woman. "You call this a house?"

"Nope," Paw drawled, "we call them shelters. You'll find they don't leak much. If yours does, just move the bed a little."

"Does he expect us to live in that?" the short woman wailed with a sort of comical expression of dismay. Whenever she spoke, she talked too loud—much too loud.

I could tell Paw was fixin' to have some fun here.

"Not unless you work for him, you don't," Paw answered. "You'll find a couple of beds in there."

"A couple!" the woman echoed. "A couple? Can't you see we got five kids, 'bout half grown, and both boys and girls?"

All the migrants sittin' there were some surprised at her outburst. Meanwhile, their kids went in to look the shelter over. "Mama, Papa!" they yelled. "Looky here! 'Tain't even finished inside, and there's nails stuck all over!"

These cabins were much like any that we had lived in—built of two-by-fours, with rough lumber round the outside. Nails were all up and down the two-by-fours on the inside, so anyone could hang up their clothes, regardless of their size. They had one old-fashioned cookstove, a table, and two chairs. The young'uns could sit on boxes or on the floor. They had two beds, one on each side of the cabin. And these cabins were quite flimsy and sittin' so close together you couldn't walk between unless you went sideways. In other words, unless you were careful, the neighbors could hear all you said. Then, like other camps, there were cheap radios blarin' all up and down the row, and dogs, cats, and kids runnin' all over. Grown folks would be yellin' greetings at each other or just passin' the time of day because they possibly haven't seen each other for mebby a year or longer and likely won't see each other again for another year. The only difference in this camp was that it was new to us and we were just gettin' acquainted.

"Well," Paw said, "I've seen six sleep in one bed— three at the head and three at the foot. The parents have a bed to themselves."

"But . . . but," stammered the thin man, "ours are boys and girls!"

"Well," Paw drawled, "they'll be sleepin', won't they?"

The man looked at Paw with dismay and then yelled, "How will I know what's goin' on? I gotta rest, don't I?"

Tim, Ben, and myself was havin' a hard time keepin' from laughin', so we went into one of the shelters, buried our faces in the blankets, and laughed and laughed. Shucks, what were these folks talkin' about? There ain't no privacy livin' in the back of a car or in a one-room shack. Heck, Tim and I had always slept, undressed, or bathed together and thought nothin' of it at all. Like I say, there just weren't no privacy at all, not none.

Havin' laughed ourselves out, we returned to the group outside.

"Well," Paw said, "you can do like we do."

"Yeah? What do you do?" inquired the thin man.

"Well," Paw said, "we work the livin' daylights out of them, whip 'em good, and then they're willin' to sleep. Fact is, I just might whip the tar out of Tim now if'n he don't get in and bring out enough coffee for all of you."

Tim, seein' the humor of it, jumped up and grabbed the seat of his pants. "Not that, Paw, not again today!" He cried as he ran to get the coffee.

Paw looked at me. "Sal," he said. "Borrow some cups so's to have enough, and bring a loaf of bread and that lunch meat."

We finally learned that the tall, thin man was named Tony, and his wife's name was Rhena. They sat silently for a few minutes, drinkin' the hot coffee. Then Tony said quietly, "Shall we go somewhere else for a job?"

The way he said it made me feel sorry for him.

"How we gonna go anywhere else, I wanta know! shouted Rhena. "There isn't enough gas in that car to wet the bottom of the tank!"

"No, guess not," said Tony weakly.

It should be stated here that every year people will come from all parts of the country because someone tells them they can make a lot of money pickin' fruit. 'Tisn't so, and it ain't fair to the people, because they aren't used to it and they know nothin' about it. Besides, there ain't a lot of money; there's hardly ever enough. It's true that Maw and Paw could make twenty dollars a day, and Tim and I could mebby pick ten dollars between us. But there was always movin' expenses. Sometimes we traveled hundreds and hundreds of miles only to learn when we reached our destination there was no work 'cause the fruit was spoiled by frost or hail or storms.

Then, sittin' on a log, Tony looked at the whole bunch of us with pleadin' in his eyes and voice. He asked, "Is it true you can make a lot of money pickin' fruit?" Then his wife came and sat next to him, facin' us.

"Depends," Paw said, "twenty dollars per day."

"See?" said Tony, turnin' to his wife. "We can make a lot." He then asked Paw, "How much can yer wife pick?"

"Well, sir, now she's a right smart picker, has always been able to keep up with me," answered Paw, lookin' at Maw with love and pride.

"That a fact?" said Tony. "Now, I know the kids don't make so much, but would you mind tellin' us what they can do?"

"Course, they're still young yet, but they'll likely make mebby ten dollars between them," said Paw.

"Well, now, that's a good deal of money," said Tony. "Why, that's right onto mebby three hundred a week. And us with five kids."

"Hold on a minute," said Paw, "just wait one tiny tick. That ain't so much money, come right down to it. Cherries won't last much more than a couple of weeks at the most, then 'twill be some time before Bartlett pears. There's your car to keep up, sometimes movin' a couple thousand miles. All takes money, you know. Right now I gotta have a set of tires, and the motor needs workin' on. No, 'taint so much. Besides I said in *good* pickin'. The cherries don't look too good this year, mebby we'll only make half that much. You asked what me and mine can do, and I told you. Because this is your first time, you most likely won't do that good. It takes time and practice to learn to be good pickers. Your young'uns—can you get them to work all day? I doubt it, as they haven't been trained. Now, these youngsters you see here has been workin' since they can remember, and that makes a difference; you had better believe it. Now, I can't go in a factory and do what you've done. Neither can you do what we do, no, not without practice."

By that time we had brought out another coffee pot full of coffee, one loaf of bread, and about a pound of sandwich meat and cups for them and their young'uns.

Settin' that in front of them, Paw said, "Better eat up—then fix yer cabin for tonight if you're gonna stay. Better split a little of that wood there. The farmer furnishes it. You'll need it to cook with in the mornin'.

Never had I seen such poor-mannered kids. They started reachin' and grabbin' till Tony backslapped one, knockin' him down. "That'll learn you manners," he said. You could tell they was thinkin' of what Paw had told them, and they didn't seem so happy no more. But eat they did, like they was a-starvin'.

Mr. Sawyer spoke up then. "Tony, mebby you and yours will catch on real quick, but 'tis hard at that. First, you put on the pickin' bag. It ties on you much like a woman's apron, and there's a round hoop, but the bottom is open. Before you go up the ladder, you bring the bottom up, and it fastens on hooks near the hoop, makin' a bottom in it. When you come down with all that weight on your neck, you must unhook the sides over your body, then the bottom opens up, pourin' the fruit in the box."

By that time, they had eaten all they had, and the coffee was about all gone. Everyone said good night, and we all went to our cabins. While Paw split wood, Tim carried it in. After the wood was split, Paw came in and said, "Darlin', what about those people?"

"Don't know, honey. They won't stick, if that's what you mean," said Maw.

"Don't mean that. I helped them carry in. Never saw no groceries. None," said Paw.

"What you want to do?" Maw asked.

Paw answered, "Don't really know. Ain't got much ourselves, but we can't let them go without, can we?"

"Hey, Paw!" Mr. Musgrove called from outside.

"Come in, come in. The door's always open," Paw answered.

After comin' in, Mr. Musgrove sat on a box by the door. "The new ones are goin' to have it hard, aren't they?" said Mr. Musgrove.

"Sure are," Paw answered. "They ain't got groceries neither."

"You sure?" asked Mr. Musgrove.

"Helped them carry in. No groceries," said Paw.

"Gonna be mighty hard on them," said Mr. Musgrove.

"Yeah," said Paw. "I been thinkin'. What's Sawyer like?"

"Well, mighty nice," said Mr. Musgrove. "Known him fer quite a spell now. He's okay."

"Tim," said Maw, "go see if Mr. Sawyer will come here a minute."

It wasn't long before the Musgrove and Sawyer families were crowded in our cabin. While us kids sat on the floor (Ben 'tween me and Tim), the grown folks sat on the only two chairs and on the edge of the beds. Must admit—it was excitin' sittin' next to Ben like I was. I had a hard time concentratin' on what was being said 'cause I was too busy makin' sure I was sittin' just right with my legs crossed just so and holdin' my hands proper. Course no one knew I was havin' this difficulty 'cause I was doin' my best, pretendin' real good that I was drawed in by all the commentin'.

"Now, then," Paw said, "we've got some people here. Ain't one of us, but they are in mighty sorry shape. What can we do for them?"

"Don't know," Mr. Sawyer said. "Really don't. Ain't none of us got much, I know, but we could let them have some taters and beans."

"We could spare some rice and flour," said Mr. Musgrove.

By the time they all got through talkin', we had gathered quite a lot of things. We had given all we could spare, like the rest. We gave them what we figured should last mebby three or four days if they'd go easy. By that time, we'd all be workin', and they could make it on their own.

After the Sawyers and Musgroves had left, Tim said, "I don't like those people, Paw. Didja notice how loud they always talk? And the way those kids were grabbin'!"

"Now, son," Paw said, "mebby they can't help it. Just mebby they were livin' by someone what was hard of hearin'. Mebby it got to be a habit. And mebby those young'uns was so hungry they just couldn't help theirselves."

"But the way they keep quarrelin' and fussin' at each other!" said Tim.

"Well," Paw said, "now they ain't used to this kind of livin'. They're havin' troubles they ain't used to, so mebby their nerves are on edge. Mebby they are real nice when they're where they belong."

"Okay, Paw," said Tim, "I'll be good to them, but I don't gotta like them, do I?"

"Son," said Paw. "We should never look at the bad in people. Remember what the good Lord said? We should love our neighbor like ourselves,"

"Oh, gosh, okay. I'll do the best I can, but it ain't gonna be easy," Tim replied good-naturedly.

That night the shelter was blazin' hot. As Paw would say, it was hotter than two billy goats fightin' in a pepper patch. The sweat rolled off my face and down my neck, and formed little puddles in the hollows of my collar bones. Maw, Paw, me, and Tim were all in our underwear sleepin' on top of the covers, Maw and Paw in one bed, and me and Tim in the other. Everyone was asleep but me. Hard as I tried, I could not go to sleep. The reason was I couldn't stop thinkin' 'bout Ben and how much fun it was talkin' with him out under the pines. Couldn't remember when I had so much fun just talkin' to some-body 'sides family. I had only been with Ben for a short space but couldn't get him outta my thoughts. I couldn't decide what it was that I liked most about him. Truth be there wasn't nothin' I didn't like 'bout him. But if I had to choose one thing I liked best, it was his smile. When he smiled, seemed like the corners of his eyes wrinkled and his dark brown eyes lit up like candles.

Then a sorrowful thought came into my mind. What was the use of even thinkin' anythin' 'bout Ben, or any other boy for that matter. Soon all the cherries would be picked, and chances was better than none that I would never ever see Ben again. And even if I did see him again, there was no way a skinny thirteen-year-old girl like me could ever hold the attention of such a fine and handsome boy like Ben. With that hurtin' thought, I closed my eyes ready to go to sleep, when I heard Rhena Griffin in the shelter next to us shout out like they was the only people in the camp—"Shut up and go to sleep!"

It musta frightened some of the dogs outside 'cause they started barkin' and howlin'. Then I heard one of their boys a-mumblin' somethin'. Then Rhena shouted back again even louder than the first. "Now what is it?"

Then I heard one of the younger children say, "It's hot in here."

Rhena didn't waste any time answerin'. "You don't think I know it's hot in here? Now shut up, all of you! Do you hear me?"

I could feel a bit of a smile formin' at the corners of my mouth. If skinny little me was hot, I could only imagine how hot Rhena musta been. In my mind I pictured her, likely in her underwear too, drippin' wet and lookin' like a plump turkey roastin' in the roastin' pan.

Then there was this long moment when no one said anythin', and then I heard Rhena say, tryin' to be real quiet so as the kids couldn't hear her. But I could hear her. She was talkin' to her husband, Tony.

"How I ever let you talk me into this I'll never know," she said.

I couldn't hear Tony say anythin'.

Then one of the kids yelled, "Git off my leg!"

Rhena musta sat up 'cause I could hear the old springs squeakin' like a bag of mice.

"Now what's the matter?"

"Horace won't stay on his side."

"Horace!" Rhena shouted. "Stay on your own side."

"That's easy for you to say," said Horace. "There's five of us in this bed, and only two of you in that one."

"Shut your mouth, Horace! Now the next person that opens his mouth is gonna sleep in the car. Do you understand?"

I could only 'magine that the whole camp was listenin' to all of this.

And then I heard what sounded like their eighteen-year-old 'cause his voice was much deeper than the others. He said, "Why didn't I think o' that?"

Then I heard more squeakin' springs and someone jumpin' off the bed onto the floor.

Then Rhena shouted again, "James! Get back in bed!"

But I figured James didn't want to listen 'cause I heard him open and slam the door real hard.

Then all of a sudden Rhena let loose with an earsplittin' scream that woke up everybody in camp and most likely their dead relatives back home.

I heard more squeakin' springs and another door a-slammin'.

Paw and Maw and me and Tim jumped out of bed, threw somethin' on, and ran outside.

One by one, all the lights went on in the shelters, and everybody and their children and dogs came runnin' to see what was the commotion.

Everybody gathered 'round Rhena, who was so hysterical that she completely forgot she was wearin' nothin' but her unmentionables. Mr. Sawyer pushed through the gatherin' and asked Rhena what seemed to be the trouble.

Far as we could make out, a mouse had been crawlin' 'cross one of them beams over Tony and Rhena's bed, and when James slammed the door, hard as he did, it jarred the whole structure and knocked the mouse off the beam, causin' the little creature to drop and land right on top of Rhena's chest.

Mr. Sawyer, doin' his darndest to keep from smilin', calmly explained that there was little field mice all over the camp, and they liked to come in at night lookin' fer somethin' to eat and that they was more 'fraid of us than we should be of them. Then Paw, with that twinkle in his eye, stepped forward and said, "I don't think you got nothin' to worry 'bout. That little feller's probably so sceered he's most likely in the next county by now."

Everyone got a good laugh over this.

And then, all at once, Rhena realized what she was wearin', or rather what she wasn't wearin'. She screamed again, covered herself best she could, and ran back into the shelter.

Ben and I had a bet—he said the Griffins wouldn't last three days. I gave them four.

SAD FAREWELL

THE NEXT MORNIN', WE WAS UP LONG BEFORE THE SUN, gettin' dressed, havin' breakfast, and readyin' ourselves for the day. We piled into the old Buick and drove to the end of the field, where all the workers parked their cars. Nearly all the cars had young babies, with the older children watchin' them, feedin' and changin' them—many times a five-year-old carin' for a tiny infant. The children didn't run up and down the cars, nor did they gather in groups, but in nearly all cases, they would just sit in the shade of their cars, a bunch of sober-faced, vacant-eyed young'uns, just watchin' and waitin' for their parents to come back to them. Cryin'? Not much. Only once in a while would you hear the tiniest one cry. They soon learned it don't do a lick o' good to cry. So all day long, they sit and wait, wait and watch, with just that sad look in their eyes—eyes that only light up when their parents come back.

The first few days are always the hardest, but that year seemed twice as bad. The heat was like a beast. By nine o'clock, it was hot; by eleven, it was like a livin' thing that invaded our bodies and seared us with a million daggers. Our arms and shoulders and legs was achin'. I could feel the sweat runnin' under my arms and down my back, then trickle down my belly. Up the ladder again. Then back down, move the ladder and go up again, all day long. Then I wondered why I didn't like bein' settled. At least bein' settled, I could just go sit somewhere. I kept tellin' myself that tomorrow it would be better. The second day always was. We wouldn't be so tired, and by the third day, it wouldn't bother us at all.

"Work faster," Tim would say. "It will stir a breeze if you go fast enough."

Twenty miles from where we was, we could see snow-covered Mount Hood, the highest mountain in all of Oregon, standin' like a sentinel, towerin' way up. All summer that snow was there. No matter how hot it was here, still that snow was there as a promise of cooler weather by and by.

Yes, there was shade in them trees, but believe me, if there was a breeze, it didn't get in there where we was pickin'. Up the ladder, fill your bucket, back down again with that weight. (With pears, apples, plums, and some citrus fruit, we used bags, but with cherries, it was buckets.) Then back up again. 'Tis true, Tim and I was only pickin' the lower limbs on eight-foot ladders, while Paw and Maw used sixteen-footers to get to the top, but still, fer young'uns like us, it was backbreakin' work. But ain't no use complainin'. We knew where the money we made from pickin' was goin'. It was goin' to pay fer the gas to get us to mebby the Imperial Valley or to Florida to pick citrus or to Arizona to pick cotton or wherever. Or it'd help with automobile repairs and food and medicine or mebby new soles for our shoes or whatever we needed. We're not just young'uns dependin' on our folks fer everythin'. No sir.

We're family, and family's fer helpin' lift the burdens of one another.

Just watchin' Maw and Paw made me wanna do my part. I was 'specially proud of frail little Maw, movin' and climbin' up and down them big ladders and workin' and workin' all day long right along with Paw, without a word o' complainin' 'bout the heat or the achin' or the bitin' flies. Oh, how those dang deer flies could bite. That's why we would try and wear long-sleeve shirts and our collars up to keep them horrible pests from bitin'.

Seems like when me and Tim got tired and wanted ta quit, Paw knew just when to catch our eye and give us a wink and a smile, lettin' us know that he loved us and was proud of the way we was workin'.

And then somethin' happened that made me soon forget 'bout the heat, the achin', and them awful, bitin' flies. As I was leanin' and stretchin' to reach a ripe bunch of cherries danglin' at the end of a branch, a cherry hit me right on top of my head. At first I thought mebby it had fallen from above, but no, it hit me much too hard to have fallen. I turned quickly in the direction from where it came but only saw Ben up in the next tree workin' real hard and wearin' the expression of a potato. Ben was just two years older than me, but he worked off the sixteen-foot ladders like his Paw and Maw. I stared at him for a long moment, but instead o' lookin' my way, he just kept on a-workin'. I went back to work, thinkin' nothin' more about it, when a moment or two later another cherry hit me—this time square in the back. I turned toward Ben again, secretly wishin' that he was the one throwin' cherries at me. But it didn't seem to be him 'cause he was still wearin' that funeral face and pickin' like there's no tomorrow. I wanted to ask him if he's the one who'd been throwin' the cherries, but I was too scared, case it wasn't him. I mean, who am I to think that a boy as old and handsome as Ben would be takin' time to be payin' interest in a girl young as me? So I turned back and began pickin' once again. Only this time I was watchin' Ben out of the corner of my eye. I can tell you, my heart nearly skipped a beat when I saw him stop pickin', slowly look down at me, and then ever so carefully take a cherry from his bucket. And then when I saw that he was just about ready to throw, I quickly turned, looked up at him, and surprised him but good.

He dropped the cherry back into his bucket and burst into a big, silly grin. I smiled back but was so unsettled by the whole thing I had to grip the ladder ever so tight so's not to fall off. What do you say when a handsome boy throws cherries at you? I was tongue tied. I could feel my face growin' hotter and hotter. Good thing my face was already red from the work and the sun, or else Ben woulda seen how bad I was blushin'. Only thing I could think of doin' right then was get down off the ladder even though my bucket was only 'bout half full. The rest of the day, Ben kept on throwin' cherries at me. I tried throwin' one back but missed him badly and nearly fell off the ladder. It was more fun than a girl's got a right.

But the new family wasn't doin' so good. I could tell just by listenin'. All day long, Tony was yellin' at his kids to get to work, only to have them yell back that it was too hot or they was too tired or too thirsty. Then Rhena, bein' so heavy and all, just gave up, sittin' in the shade eatin' part of what was picked. I guess Tony'd had enough, 'cause he got down off his ladder and started chasin' after two of his teenage boys and shoutin' at them, "Get back up those ladders and get to work, you lazy good-fer-nothin's!"

As the boys ran, they shouted back, "It's too hot!" and "We wanna go home!"

There was no way Tony could catch the boys. I felt real sorry for him. He had been in one of the trees next to me, and I could see how hard and fast he was tryin' to pick.

He was fed up and walked toward Rhena. We could see from where we was that Rhena's lips were stained all red from eatin' the cherries.

All the workers stopped workin' and held their breath. We watched from our ladders as Tony slowly walked toward Rhena. It wasn't hard to tell that Tony was spittin' mad. He stopped and looked down at her. His big hands closed, tightened, then turned into fists, all white.

"I've had it tryin' to get everybody to work," he said. Rhena didn't even look up. She just popped another cherry in her mouth like she couldn't care less, then said, as she was fishin' another cherry from the bucket. "What do you want me to do about it?"

Tony had reached his boilin' point.

"I want you to get off your fat can and get back up that ladder and help me make some money! That's what I want you to do about it."

When Tony said this, all the workers gasped, made big eyes, and formed the letter "O" with their mouths. After'n what Tony said, Rhena's eyes went black as a skillet. She slowly got to her feet and started toward Tony. I believe poor Tony was havin' second thoughts 'bout what he had said, 'cause he started slowly backin' away.

"Don't you ever talk to me like that again, you long string of spit!" shouted Rhena. "If you remember, I never wanted to come here in the first place!"

And then she wound up and threw a cherry at Tony. It was a perfect strike, hittin' him square in the forehead. And she kept throwin' them. Tony turned and started runnin', with Rhena behind him throwin' and shoutin'. As she chased him, we laughed so hard we nearly fell off our ladders.

None of us won our bet. Tony and Rhena and their family left for West Virginia that very night. I can't say that I blame 'em. They made only fifteen dollars 'tween them compared to our sixty. Before they left, the workers scraped together enough money for gas to get them all the way home. On top of that, they filled their trunk with coffee, taters, lunch meat, beans, and whatever else they could find. That was the way of the migrant. If they had more than what they needed, somebody else should have it. I have never forgotten the Griffins. They made me proud that I was a migrant.

One night, a silly, puzzlin' thing happened to me, makin' me realize just how much I cared what Ben thought of me. I was in the shelter helpin' Maw get supper on when Tim and Ben came runnin', wantin' to know if I wanted to join in a game that all the other children were playin'. I could tell Maw was 'specially tired that night, so I told them I couldn't go 'cause Maw needed help. Right then I knew Maw was truly tired, 'cause another time she woulda told me to run along and have fun. Anyhow, as I stood there lookin' at Ben, suddenly I became mindful that I was barefooted, and worst of all, my big feet were black with dirt. Ashamed and embarrassed, I plopped one foot top the other and stayed thata way till Ben and Tim left. After they left, I told Maw what I was feelin', and she told me when you like someone, you always wanna look, act, and be your very best when they're around you. And what's more, she said you should choose someone who makes you want to be your best. From there on out, I decided I would try to look and be the best I could, 'specially when I was 'round Ben.

Sadly, all too soon, the cherries were picked, and it was time to be movin' on. The season was a good one, and our friendships with the Musgroves, Sawyers, and some of the other families became solid. For me it seemed it was the shortest season possible, and worst of all, it would be at least a whole year till I saw Ben again. I just didn't know how I was gonna say good-bye to him. When we wasn't workin' or sleepin', we was in the pines climbin' trees, playin' hide and seek, or swimmin' in the creek. Paw said we was headin' to Florida to pick citrus, Sawyers was goin' to the Imperial Valley, while the Musgroves wasn't too sure where they would go—mebby to Phoenix, Arizona.

The mornin' we was leavin' found me and Ben alone beneath the pines. My heart felt heavy and sad. Sayin' good-bye to good friends is always a sad thing. 'Specially when you may never see them again. We was just standin' 'long the creek, tossin' pebbles in and talkin'. "Sure gonna miss this place," I said.

"Me too," said Ben.

"Can't already wait for next summer."

"Me neither," said Ben.

Just 'bout then, I heard Tim callin'. I looked out to the open field that separated the pines from the shelters and could see Tim mebby fifty yards away.

"Sal!" he shouted. "Paw says it's time to be a-gettin' and a-goin'."

I shouted back. "Tell Paw I'm comin'."

"Good-bye, Ben!" shouted Tim. "See you next year."

Ben waved good-bye, and Tim turned and ran back toward the shelters.

I tried not lookin' at Ben, knowin' that any minute the tears were gonna start gushin' out. Tryin' to control my tender and fragile feelin's best I could, I looked away and said, "I think the thing I'm gonna miss the most about this place is . . . *you!*" And then I did the boldest thing I ever done in all my thirteen years. I reached up, grabbed Ben by his ears, pulled his face to mine, and kissed him! Yes! I kissed him right on his lips! If there was a contest who had the biggest eyes at that very moment, I think 'tween me and Ben, Ben woulda won hands down.

I could feel the dam about to break and the flood waters a-comin', so I wasted no time, turnin' 'round and runnin' fast as I could out of the pines and into the big field. When I got mebby fifty yards away where Ben could no longer see my tears, my runnin' nose, and my red, blotchy face, I turned 'round and shouted, "Good-bye! See you next summer." And then I said it. I still can't believe I said it. "I love you!"

I was only thirteen, and Ben was only fifteen, but I did love him. I saw Ben break into a big smile. Then, all embarrassed like, I turned, lifted my skirt, and ran fast as I could through the tall grass back to the shelters.

Six

THIRTY-ONE-CENT MIRACLE

LEAVIN' HOOD RIVER AND GOIN' SOUTH, YOU CLIMB UP AND up till you are several hundred feet above the giant pines, lookin' way, way down on the trees. Once we got to the top and started down the far side, we were goin' faster and faster.

"Slow down, honey," Maw said.

"Can't," Paw said. "Our brakes are gone!"

To prove it, he stepped on the brake several times, and each time he did, the pedal banged against the floor boards. He tried to put it in a lower gear, but the car was goin' too fast. All's Paw could do was put it in high and shut off the motor.

What happened next is hard to explain.

Maw said, "Lordy, Lordy!" and she stamped her foot like she was hopin' the Lord would put a brake on her side. As the tires made awful screechin' sounds around the curves, I looked over the edge. I could just see us a-tumblin' head over heels and just knew that this was the end.

"Are we gonna crash, Paw?" Tim asked.

"Can't tell," Paw shouted. "Let you know later."

Now, Paw was tryin' to be calm, but I could see the beads of sweat on his forehead.

He didn't grip the wheel nor hunch over but just sat back. It seemed that only his fingers were touchin' the wheel—like he was part of the car and the car was part of him, and both was lookin' out for each other.

Again, Maw stamped like mebby a brake was there.

"Do somethin', honey, do somethin'!" she begged.

"I am," Paw said as we careened around the next curve. "I'm prayin'."

"You scared?" I said to Tim as we laid on the back seat.

"Shucks," Tim replied, his eyes alight with excitement. "Paw's drivin', ain't he?"

Then the next curve we took on two wheels. I felt the car tip up, then settle back. And then just as we screeched around another curve, we saw a sign ahead that read, "Road for Runaway Trucks." Looked like Paw's prayer was bein' answered. Straight ahead was a cut in the side of the mountain with a dirt road climbin' straight up. It was just a dirt road, but it looked like heaven to us. 'Twas cut there for trucks out of control. We hit the straight away, goin' uphill, and as soon as we rolled to a stop, Maw said, "Praise the Lord!"

We went clear to bottom of the mountain in low gear. In the first town we came to, we bought a new cylinder for the brakes.

If it had been just the brakes, we woulda been all right. But the water pump went kaput in Colorado. Then, crossin' Kansas, we blew a tire. By the time we got halfway through Missouri, we had to replace the alternator. By then we were countin' our nickels. When we got to Alabama, we were down to our last thirty cents.

We arrived at the edge of Goodwater, Coosa County,

Alabama, at about one o'clock in the afternoon on a Sunday. Paw pulled the old Buick up in front of a respectable restaurant—Big Mama's Truck Stop was the name of it.

"Gonna stop here," said Paw.

I turned to Tim and asked, "Why's Paw stoppin' at a nice place like Big Mama's when we're so broke?"

All's Tim could do was shrug his shoulders.

Right then a big, fancy, open convertible pulled in next to us on the driver's side.

Tim's eyes nearly popped when he saw the car. "Paw! Look at that car!"

Paw eyed the car, then said, "That's a Cadillac, son. A Cadillac eight. One of the finest automobiles you'll ever see, mebby in your entire life."

I wasn't lookin' at the car; I was lookin' at the dress the pretty young girl in the backseat was wearin'. I reckon she was most likely a year or two younger than me. Her dress was all frilly and whiter than anythin' I had ever laid eyes on. Her blonde hair was in ringlets and pink ribbons. She looked like somethin' out of one of those New York magazines. When the family got out of the car, I could see they was all dressed proper like they had just come from attendin' church services.

I couldn't help myself and stuck my head out the window and called out to the girl in the frilly dress. "That sure is a pretty dress."

The little girl smiled and was 'bout to say somethin', but the girl's mother, with a goody-two-shoes look all over her face, took her by the arm and pulled her toward the entrance of the restaurant.

"Maw," I said, "did you see the dress on that girl?"

Maw was starin' out her window, actin' like somethin' was botherin' her. "Yes, darlin', I saw it. It is a beauty."

Paw, unawares of what we was talkin' 'bout, dug into his pocket, took out his change, and began countin' it.

"Paw?" I asked. "Are those respectable folks?"

"'Bout as respectable as you can get, I s'pose."

Soon as Paw finished countin' his change, he said, "Everybody ready?"

That was when Maw turned from her window and looked at Paw with a solemn and serious expression on her face. "I don't wanna go in there, Paw. We're broke, and besides, it's Sunday and we're not dressed proper."

"We're not broke, darlin'. We got ourselves thirty cents."

Then Tim, from the backseat, says with eternal optimism, "I gotta penny!"

Paw chuckled and said, "There you have it—thirty-one cents."

Maw turned away again, stared out her window, and said, "Can't buy nothin' with thirty-one cents."

Paw dropped his thirty cents in his shirt pocket and looked over at Maw. "You might be surprised, darlin', just how far thirty-one cents will go in these parts. Don't forget what the good Lord did with the fishes and the loaves. After all those people were fed and full, there was twenty-eight baskets of leftovers. Imagine that."

"Twenty-eight baskets!" exclaimed Tim. "How is that possible, Paw?"

Paw unlatched the door and said, "'Twas a miracle, son. Now, c'mon everybody."

As Paw held the door open to Big Mama's, Maw walked 'head of me. I couldn't help noticin' how straight and proud she walked, with her hair to her shoulders, all fluffed out like Paw liked it. She seemed so proud, and I wondered, what we got to be proud of? Just as we entered, I heard a man say, "Snowballs."

Paw heard him and said, "You got that right, mister." He said it like he was bein' honored or somethin'. I must admit I felt ashamed, because 'twas the same as callin' us fruit tramps. The man that said that was sittin' on a stool at the end of the counter that ran along one side of the place. The family in the fine car was seated at a table in the center. I knew right off that the woman behind the counter had to be Big Mama 'cause she was one of the biggest women I'd ever seen. She musta been 'bout five foot nine inches tall and weighed mebby two hundred fifty pounds.

I thought we would sit in a booth so as all couldn't hear what we ordered. But no, Paw, carin' less as always 'bout what people thought, didn't go to no booth but straight to the counter, like he owned the place. Paw sat on a stool, with Maw on his left, Tim on his right, and me next to Tim.

Well, Big Mama came over with water. "Care for a menu?" she asked. "No, ma'am," Paw said. "Reckon no." He didn't talk any different than he ever did. "Just two coffees," he said, like he was orderin' a turkey dinner all around, cost no object.

Big Mama's eyes opened wide in surprise, and her forehead wrinkled as she repeated, "Two coffees?"

"You heard me right. That is correct," said Paw.

Lookin' in the mirror on the wall behind the counter, I could see a couple in one of the booths lookin' at us and whisperin'. I watched my face turnin' red before duckin' my head to stare at the counter.

"Hold on a minute!" Paw said.

Big Mama turned back from enterin' the kitchen.

"How much is yer toast?" asked Paw.

"One dime," she said.

"Okay, then, bring the coffee when the toast is ready and two extra glasses please," Paw requested.

I can tell you everyone in the whole place was silent—and I was so ashamed, because we didn't belong there with all them respectable folks.

As she brought the coffee, Big Mama leaned on the counter in front of Maw and Paw, not knowin' quite who to give the toast to.

"Will that be all, sir?" asked Big Mama.

"Reckon so, ma'am," Paw answered with a poker face. "Never order more than I can pay fer."

And I knew she would begin to ask a million questions, like where are y'all goin' and so on. Everybody always did.

Sure enough, as she sat the toast in front of Paw, she asked, "What's the matter? Broke?"

"No, ma'am," Paw answered as he shoved the toast to Tim, who shoved it to me. "Got enough to pay for this," he continued.

In so sayin', he carefully laid down one dime, two nickels, and ten pennies. Then he said to Tim, "You'll have to give her yer penny fer tax."

Tim took the penny out of his pocket and slid it down the counter to Paw.

Now, we had been taught that we must always share and share alike, whether it's work, food, or play. So, carefully cuttin' the two slices of toast, I kept half a piece for myself, then passed the rest to Tim, who, in turn, took his half piece then passed what was left to Paw and Maw. Watchin' all this, Big Mama's eyebrows went way up.

"Where you from?" she asked quietly.

"Washington," Paw said.

"These your young'uns?" she asked

"Yes, ma'am."

Lots o' folks asked Paw and Maw that very question, 'cause like I said, they looked too old to have children young as us. Paw always said that it took him long as it did to get hitched 'cause it took that long to find hisself the perfect, most beautiful woman in the country. Lookin' at Maw, I knew there was a lot o' truth to what Paw was sayin' 'cause she was as pretty and good through and through as they come.

Maw and Paw poured half their coffee into the extra glasses and passed them on to me and Tim. Course, Big Mama was watchin' all this with great interest.

"Where you headed?" Big Mama asked.

Oh, why don't she go away? I thought to myself. *Ain't she got nothin' else to do but ask questions? 'Tain't none of her business. We ain't askin' fer nothin', are we? All we did was buy what we could. Why don't Paw tell her to mind her own business?*

But Paw, lookin' straight in her eyes with that steady way of lookin', said, "Florida."

"Live there?" was her next question.

"No, ma'am," Paw drawled, pointin' his thumb to the guy settin' on the stool almost next to me, and continuin', "They call us snowballs in Florida. Central states calls us migrant workers—that is, the north central—while the western states call us fruit tramps. That's us." Paw nodded and was lookin' at her like he was proud of it.

"Why don't you quit that and settle down?" she asked curiously.

"Have thought 'bout it," Maw interrupted, "but then I wonder who would train yer hops, block yer beets, pick yer fruit?"

Big Mama thought 'bout that for a moment, then said, "Let someone else do it."

"Yep," said Maw, "but what if we all quit? Then what? Isn't that kinda askin' why everyone don't study electronics?"

As Maw said that, the one who called us snowballs walked out, kind of lookin' like he was ashamed.

I jumped as a boomin' voice from behind said, "That's right, missus, you tell 'em!"

'Twas the man in the booth with the woman.

"Does me good to see you folks stand up fer your job," he said, "so many of you people seem ashamed. But you keep on goin', mister, you can be as proud as the next."

It turned out that Big Mama's heart was as big and soft as she was. When she saw Tim pressin' his fingers hard on his plate makin' sure he got up every last crumb, she slowly shook her head, then disappeared into the kitchen.

It wasn't long before Big Mama and her cook came out of the back carryin' four big chicken dinners with mashed taters, vegetables, and hot rolls and set them down on the counter in front of us. I don't think I will ever taste anythin' that delicious again. After we finished our dinners, Big Mama brought out for each of us a large piece of cherry pie. I must admit the cherry pie made me think of pickin' cherries, but most of all, Ben. I could picture Ben's dark eyes a-sparklin' when he smiled. I wondered where he was and what he must be doin'. I was anxious to get a-goin' because just as soon as we got busy workin' again, time would pass quickly, and soon it would be cherry pickin' time in Hood River.

When we left, Big Mama sent us on our way with the biggest lunch I had ever seen. She waved good-bye to us from the porch of her restaurant. We waved back through the rear window until we couldn't see her no more. The lunch lasted us for nearly two days, and when we finished it, we found a twenty-dollar bill at the bottom of the bag along with a note that read, "Good luck," and it was affectionately signed by Big Mama. From that day forth, we always called that day at Big Mama's truck stop our thirty-one-cent miracle.

One night, as dark was settlin' in, we camped on a barren hill overlookin' a small town somewhere in eastern Alabama. Tim built a fire, and I cooked taters in the skillet. I could tell somethin' was botherin' Maw. She seemed distant and troubled. She said she wasn't hungry, then left the campfire and walked to the edge of the hill, mebby thirty feet from where our fire was, and just stared down at the town.

As Paw took his last bite, he said to me, "Sal, darlin', can't remember when I've tasted taters this good."

"Thanks, Paw," I said.

Then Tim looked at Maw and asked Paw, "What's troublin' her, Paw? She's been like that all day. It's not like her to be actin' this way."

"Not sure, son," said Paw, gettin' to his feet. "You young'uns go ahead and clean up, and I'll go have a talk with her."

Tim and me were curious to know what was botherin' Maw, so we tried to be extra quiet as we cleaned up.

'Twasn't right to be pryin' in on our folks' conversation, but we were family, and we wanted to know what was troublin' Maw so as to know what we could do to cheer her up.

"What is it, Maw?" we heard Paw say. "What is it that's botherin' you?"

Maw didn't look at Paw but kept starin' down at the houses and buildin's below. After a while, she answered, "I'm tired of us bein' bums, Paw. I wanna settle down and be like respectable folks again."

When I heard Maw say "settle," I felt my heart sink. I wanted to shout, "Tell her no, Paw!" *Why was Maw talkin' like this?* I wondered. And then it came to me like a flash. It was them people with the big car and the nice clothes that got to Maw. Oh, why did I have to notice that fancy dress on that girl? But worst of all, why did I have to bring Maw's attention to it? It was all makin' sense now—why Maw just looked out the window and didn't want to go into Big Mama's. I put the skillet in the trunk where we always put it, then sat down on the runnin' board of the Buick and listened some more.

"But we're happy bums, ain't we?" I heard Paw ask Maw. I could tell by the way he said it that he was smilin' and tryin' to cheer her. "That's gotta count for somethin', don't it?"

Maw looked up at Paw and said, "Our young'uns should be sittin' at a table eatin' their supper instead of sittin' on the ground in front of a fire and livin' outta the trunk of a car their whole lives."

Paw put his arm around Maw's shoulder, pulled her in close, and said, "They're just as happy—"

But Maw cut him off real quick like. "Because they

don't know better!" Then she took in a deep breath and looked up at Paw again. "Paw," she said, and she said it the way she always did when she really wanted somethin', which was not very oft.

I was feelin' hopeless 'cause when Maw really, really wanted somethin', Paw always gave in 'cause he loved her so.

Maw's voice was all spirited and hopeful. "We could grow a garden, Paw, and have our own vegetables and fruit and then can it all in the fall. Sal needs to learn how to do things like cannin' and keepin' a house. We could have a yard with grass for the kids to play in, and they could go to a real school and have them a proper education. We could go to church on Sundays and worship like we should. Our young'uns could grow up like normal, respectable people."

I wanted to run to Maw and shout out, "No! We are not goin' to settle down!" But I couldn't. 'Twouldn't be right. We were taught to always be respectful of our elders, and that would not be respectful. But the last thing I wanted was to settle. I wanted to travel and see the country and meet new people and do all the things respectable children don't ever get to do. But if the truth were known, the real reason I didn't want to settle down was that if we did, I may never see Ben again. And I couldn't bear that.

Then I heard Paw say, "In my way of thinkin', darlin', being like respectable folks ain't exactly what I had in mind for this family."

Good fer you, Paw, I thought to myself. *Stick by your guns, Paw.* But then I heard Maw say, "It's what I want, Paw." The way she said it, all determined like, I knew that was the end of their talkin'.

Later, around the fire, me and Tim tried to persuade

Maw that we wouldn't be happy settlin' down. But Maw wouldn't hear a word of it. She said we were just young'uns and didn't know what was best. That's why young'uns have maws and paws.

That night I cried myself to sleep.

Seven

RESPECTABLE FOLKS

WHEN WE WAS TRAVELIN' THROUGH EASTERN IOWA ONE
year ago last summer, we met a farmer named Lourie who
offered Paw a job and a five-room house to live in. Course
Paw turned it down at the time, but, just in case, Paw kept
Lourie's information in the car's glove box. Paw was able
to reach him by telephone and found out that Lourie had
need of help. So we headed north. It took us 'bout a week
to reach Iowa. Normally it doesn't take that long, but we
ran out of money and had to stop along the way and do
odd jobs for gas and food. We cleaned out horse stalls and
pig pens and even put a roof on a chicken coop.

It was on a Friday afternoon in the late fall when we
arrived in the small town of Palo. Palo was not too far
from Cedar Rapids. I didn't much like Iowa. It was just
too dang flat. I yearned to see mountains like we had
seen in the West and Northwest. I 'specially missed seein'
snow-covered Mount Hood.

Mr. Lourie told us he knew where we could buy fur-
niture at a second-hand store, and they would trust us to
pay mebby five dollars or so a week. Well, Paw would be
makin' a hundred and seventy-five dollars per month, and

besides, Mr. Lourie would give us a hog to butcher and two quarts of milk per day.

Mr. Lourie went ahead of us in his truck, took us to the store, and told the man to fix us up.

"Now," Paw told Maw, "we won't buy only what we gotta have, then we won't owe so much. We can buy more later."

Course we needed everythin': stoves, both heatin' and cookin', a vacuum machine, a table, chairs, and so on. But after we had all we had to have, Paw says, "Darlin', 'tain't every day we go shoppin'; now you pick out somethin' you want." That's how come Maw got the Birdseye maple vanity set for just twenty-two dollars.

Course, we didn't have to have the record player, but 'tis nice to have, so we got that. Then a bicycle for Tim, 'cause he never had one and it was only eight dollars. So then I needed somethin', so I got a mother-of-pearl mirror and brush and comb set and three dresses fer only five dollars. Well, countin' the washin' machine, it came to a little over two hundred dollars. But shucks, only eight dollars per week, and we'd be makin' money hand over fist. Gosh, right around forty dollars every week!

Right at that time, we didn't even have enough money to flag down a boxcar, so we had to borrow thirty dollars from the boss for groceries. Had to have lights turned on, so that was another six dollars, and coal at eighteen dollars. All-in-all, we were head over heels in debt. I guess that was what made us respectable people.

Eight

FEEDIN' THE SHEEP

WE LIVED AND WORKED IN IOWA FOR MORE THAN A YEAR. Sadly, we did not make it back to Hood River for cherry pickin', but I never quit prayin' and hopin' that I would see Ben again.

We worked hard that year. Mr. Lourie turned out to be a good boss—fair and honest. Even let us plant one of his acres. In the spring, Paw turned the ground, and Maw, me, and Tim planted tomatoes, squash, rows and rows of corn, pumpkins, melons, beans, and even potatoes. All summer long, Tim and me, as it was our job, weeded and watered and watched things grow. 'Twas a miracle to see tiny little seeds with a little water and a whole lot o' sunshine start sproutin' tiny little plants up out of the ground, then keep on a-growin' and a-growin' till that whole acre was burstin' with all kinds of vegetables. At summer's end and into the fall, we harvested and preserved the fruit and vegetables for winter. With each bottle placed on the shelf, I cried a tear because it meant that we would be stayin' that much longer in Iowa. A day didn't go by that I didn't think about Ben, wonderin' what he was doin' and fearful that he might meet someone new. Each night before goin' to sleep, I would try and picture him in my mind—the way he looked and the way he talked. But sadly, the more time that passed made me forget, and time just kept rollin' by.

Paw went to work at six and came home at six. At summer's end, we went to school every day of the week, and then on Sunday it was always our habit to worship with the rest of the farmers and their hired help. Just two miles down the road was a little white chapel with a steeple settin' on top. Mostly about thirty people came each Sunday to worship. We all cleaned up real good on Saturday nights. Maw would wash, iron, and starch Paw's and Tim's shirts and mine and her dress and rag tie my hair in curls so it would be special for Sunday. We loved goin' to church, but then somethin' happened one Sunday mornin' that was the cause of us never goin' back.

The minister was preachin' that mornin' from the book of Matthew in the New Testament, chapter twenty-five. He was a large man with a great boomin' voice.

"For I was an hungered and ye gave me meat . . ."

I leaned forward and looked at the minister's stomach. From where I was sittin', he didn't look all that hungered. His stomach was droopin' over his belt like a batch of bread dough that was left too long and had raised so much that it was hangin' over the bread pan. I took a look at skinny little Paw sittin' right beside me, so thin from all his workin' he had to take a nail and hammer and make three more holes in his belt just so's he could keep his pants from fallin' down. Even so, he had the habit of yankin' on them every minute or so to keep them up.

As the minister kept on a-readin'—"I was naked and ye clothed me."—I couldn't help but notice Paw's clothes.

His shoe was split wide open at the sole, and I could see his big toe peekin' out where his sock was worn clear through. His trousers looked 'bout the same—one knee worn clear through and the other so thin you could 'bout read a newspaper through it. I leaned forward to get a look at what the minister was wearin'. His shoes looked bran' spankin' new and so did everythin' else he was wearin'. All of this got me to thinkin' and gave me a good idea. Mebby Paw ought to start preachin'. It sure would be a lot easier than what he was doin' everyday, and he could be makin' a whole lot more. When we were travelin' around the country, Paw was our preacher, and I sure did like the way he preached better 'n this preacher.

All of a sudden, the minister shouted out, "FEED MY SHEEP!" The ones that were asleep woke up real fast like, and the ones who was already awake or half asleep got the gajeebies scared right out of them.

The minister looked down at a little gray-haired man and said, "Brother Smith, would you be so kind as to help me?"

Brother Smith took an empty cigar box off the bench and got to his feet. Everyone knew it was time to get out their billfolds. All the farmers, includin' Paw began to drop dollar bills and coins into the cigar box. As this was goin' on, the minister said, "Don't ever tighten your purse strings against the Lord. But leave the purse strings loose so the Lord can reach in now and then as He needs to." As the box began fillin', he kept repeatin' hisself, "Oh, thank you, thank you, thank you."

Me and Tim was watchin' real close, tryin' to keep a runnin' count of the money as it was bein' dropped into the box. We figured the congregation must have contributed at least two hundred bobs. Why, that was more than Paw made workin' two hundred and forty hours a month for Mr. Lourie! For certain we were gonna get Paw to start preachin'.

On the way home, Tim leaned over the front seat and asked, "Hey Paw, what does that preacher man do with all that money he collects?"

"Well," Paw said, "I s'pose some goes for expenses to keep the church a-goin', and then I reckon the rest goes to the preacher for preachin'."

"Why don't you start preachin', Paw?" I asked. "You could preach a whole lot better 'n him."

I could tell Maw agreed 'cause she looked at Paw all admirin' like, smilin' and a-noddin'.

"Yeah, Paw," said Tim. "Why doncha start preachin'? Sure would be lot easier than workin' for Mr. Lourie."

"If the truth be told," answered Paw, "I couldn't do it 'cause I would have a hard time takin' of the Lord."

Just then, Paw spotted somethin' off the side of the road. It was a travel-worn Plymouth that had pulled off the paved highway and was parked on a narrow dirt road next to a cornfield. Paw hit the brakes, made a U-turn, took the side road, and pulled in behind the Plymouth.

"Can I come, Paw?" I asked.

"Come along, darlin'."

We got out of the car and moved to the Plymouth. Paw and me knew right off that this was a migrant family. Could tell by the way the car was packed—everythin' in its place. A man and woman what looked like in their forties was in the front seat. Behind them, sittin' in the backseat was a girl 'bout seventeen and a boy 'bout eighteen. The girl was holdin' a tiny little newborn baby. The baby was cryin', and the girl didn't look so good. She was all pale, weary, and worn out.

"Folks havin' trouble?" Paw asked.

Soon we learned that the young gal had just given birth two days before, and she and the baby were ailin' and feverish. They needed a doctor awful bad but were flat busted broke. They told us they had stopped just moments before we arrived to say a prayer askin' for help. Well, that was all Paw needed to hear. He paused and thought for a long moment after he heard this. I could see in his eyes that he was feelin' a tender stirrin' inside, and I knew why. Paw was a firm believer that the way the good Lord answers prayers is through other folks, and he knew it was no accidental happenin' that he saw those folks parked where they was. There was no doubt in his mind that he was s'posed to be the answer to their prayer. Same as the day Paw saw Ben fightin' for his life in the great Columbia. Can't tell me Ben wasn't pleadin' and beggin' the Lord to save him just before Paw happened to turn his head at that most convenient time.

Anyway, Paw took his billfold from his back pocket and emptied it, givin' them poor folks every bob in it. Next he started emptyin' his pockets of what coins he had, when somethin' distracted his eyes. He turned, looked up on the highway, and saw the minister there stopped and lookin' in our direction.

Paw, lickety-split like, 'scused himself, then ran fast as he could up to where the minister's car was and began explainin' the trouble the poor family was havin'. As the minister was lookin' down at the Plymouth and listenin' to Paw, somethin' on the backseat of the car caught Paw's attention. It was the bag of collection money collected of the farmers and workers at church that day.

The minister turned back to Paw, looked at his wrist watch, said he wished he could help, then made some 'scuse about bein' late for a meetin'. Then he put the car in gear and drove off, but not before Paw was able to slip his hand inside the open back window and snatch away that bag of collection money. Paw hid it behind his back so as the minister couldn't see it in his rearview mirror. When Paw figured it was safe, he looked up toward heaven and said, "Forgive me, Father, but You've got some sheep down here that need feedin' real bad."

Paw said he was only gonna dip into the bag and take out a little, but the purse strings were tied so tight that he couldn't. He figured it was the Lord's way o' tellin' him to give all of it to the migrants.

'Bout a good mile down the road, the minister noticed the bag of money missin', slammed on the brakes, turned around, and raced back. When he got back, the migrants were long gone.

That night, people from the church came by the house lookin' all stern and serious and self-righteous. Paw told 'em straight out what he had done and why he done it. What Paw told them didn't matter any. They told Paw they wanted the money. Paw said he would pay it all back, and he kept his promise. It took Paw four months to pay back every red cent, 'cept, of course, what he had put into the cigar box hisself. We never went back to that church. Hypocrites, Paw called them. From that day on, Paw was the only preacher we ever knew.

At first being settled wasn't so bad. When Paw came home, he would start soundin' the car horn soon as he left the highway and kept it goin' all the way down the dirt

road till he got to the house. We would all come a-runnin'
when we heard it. Paw would get out of the car and hug
Maw and hug us kids, and then we would spend the rest
of the night together havin' supper, listenin' to the radio or
record player. As time went by, though, we began missin'
our old life. Even seemed like Maw and Paw began to get
restless and itchin' to be a-gettin' and a-goin.'

Nine

A-GETTIN' AND A-GOIN'

THEN ONE NICE DAY IN THE MIDDLE OF JULY, I WAS OUT BY the old woodshed, sittin' on a pile of wood, when Tim walked up to me and asked, "How you like bein' settled?"

"Hate it," I said. "Just sittin' in one place, never goin' nowhere. Gosh, we might as well be a tree or somethin'. Besides, the kids at school ain't all that smart. Least don't seem so. Gosh, they don't know where nothin' is 'cept by lookin' in a book. They ain't got no idea how far it really is from one place to 'nother."

"Even sometimes," said Tim, "I think we know the lay of the land better than our teacher."

"Gosh, Tim," I said, "I wish we could be a-gettin' and a-goin' again. Seems like all my insides are cryin' to go. 'Tis like a sickness. If I was older, I'd just start walkin' and keep right on walkin'. Maw ain't so happy either. Notice how she stands so much in front of the window, just lookin' and lookin'?"

"'Tain't much fun ridin' the bicycle anymore," said Tim. "Heck, just up and down the road. Ain't nothin' to it. No one listens to the radio no more. The record player ain't been played for ever so long. And the old swing just hangs and hangs there. Besides, ain't hardly no trees 'round here, not in these parts, anyhow. Nothin' but flat, flat ground everywhere you look. The biggest hill is only 'bout ankle high."

Tim was right. For miles and miles, all's you could see were plowed fields with cattle corrals here, there, and everywhere. And the wind last winter cut across here like crazy, pilin' snow up higher and higher 'cause there weren't no windbreak at all.

"Ain't nothin' to do here either," complained Tim. "What can I do but carry in a little coal and empty a few ashes? 'Tain't like gettin' out and workin' 'longside your folks. And Paw don't come home so happy no more either. He just comes and sits on the porch and stares off till Maw calls supper."

Way far off, I could see a storm buildin' and comin' toward us. "We better go in now, Tim," I said. "The storm will soon hit here. 'Sides, it's 'bout time for Paw."

As we walked in, Maw was standin' by the window, starin' out with vacant eyes. She just stood there, lookin' and lookin'. I don't think she even knew we came in. So we just lay on the floor, not sayin' nothin'.

From one window to another, Maw paced 'round that room like an animal in a cage. It weren't long 'fore Paw walked in. No sense runnin' to him, not anymore. He'd just brush our hair with his hand, then walk outside and sit on the porch. This time he just came in, not sayin' nothin', and sat down in the rocker.

Thick, rollin' clouds was overhead now makin' the house dark. Every few seconds lightnin' would flash and thunder would bang, causin' the house to tremble 'round us. No one turned on the lights. Me and Tim still lay where we were. Paw was sittin' and rockin' back and forth slowly. Maw was still lookin' and lookin', only she can't see nothin' 'cept the lightnin'.

"Want some coffee, Paw?" Maw asked.

"Not now," was the only answer she got from him.

This wasn't the first night like this. It happened quite often now. Finally we'll eat and go to bed. But this night, Maw said, "Hon, soon be cherry pickin' time in Hood River."

"Yes, darlin', cherry pickin' time," Paw said.

There was silence fer a long spell. Then Paw said, "We'd usually be there by now. But we're respectable folks."

"Yes, honey, respectable," said Maw.

After more silence, I squeezed Tim's hand. We looked at each other and smiled and kept on a-listenin'.

Maw sighed gently and said "'Twas kinda fun, wasn't it, Paw?"

"Sure was, just goin' and goin'. Workin' the fruit. But we're respectable folks now," said Paw.

"Would be a good night for goin'. I like travelin' in a storm," Maw said thoughtfully.

"Me too," said Paw.

I squeezed Tim's hand again and whispered, "Bet they'll go."

"Sure they will," he whispered. "They're talkin', ain't they?'"

"Wonder where our friends are and what they're doin'," Paw said.

"Wish I knew, honey," said Maw. "I feel like we're lettin' them down."

There was a long pause. Finally Maw said, "Let's go, Paw. I'm tired of bein' so respectable. The boss won't care.

We paid him all back and don't owe him nothin'." She said it with more life in her voice than we'd heard for many a day.

Just then a great flash of lightnin' lit the room up like it was the middle of the day. And then thunder exploded. The house shook, and the windows rattled. It seemed to knock Paw right out of the rocker. He hurried 'cross the room and flipped on the lights, then looked at us children. "What's the matter with you young'uns?" he asked, his eyes smilin'. "Don't you know that was the good Lord a-tellin' us that it's time to be a-gettin' and a-goin'?"

The whole family was runnin' back and forth from the house loadin' the car. It was rainin' like the dickens, but heck, we didn't care. We were laughin' and havin' the time of our lives. Thirty minutes later, we were all packed and ready to go. When Paw, last one to get into the car, closed the door, he looked at us kids, then at Maw. It was a moment I can never forget. Our hair was soppin' wet, and the rain was runnin' down our faces and drippin' off our noses. All's we could hear was the poundin' rain hittin' the roof of the car. We just looked at each other wide eyed and smilin' all silly like. Even if we wanted to, we couldn't have stopped smilin'. Then Paw put his hand on Maw's shoulder and said, "Be a good darlin' and pour a cup o' coffee. Believe we could all enjoy one now."

While the windshield wipers seemed to say, "Hurry up—hurry up," we drank our coffee. Later, as Tim and I laid down and covered up with a blanket, the wipers still kept sayin', "Hurry up—hurry up." We fell asleep listenin' to them and to Maw and Paw singin' "Draw Me Nearer."

I am thine, Oh Lord, I have heard Thy voice,
And it told Thy love to me;

But I long to rise in the arms of faith
And be closer drawn to Thee . . .

After'n that, we never wanted to settle and be respectable folks again.

Ten

RETURN TO HOOD RIVER

THE NEXT DAY PAW SENT A POSTCARD TO MR. JOHNSON tellin' him that we was on our way to Hood River and to make sure he saved us a shelter to stay in. Paw drove steady for two whole days and one night, never once sleepin' a wink. 'Tis true that most migrant women do drive to help their men, but Maw never learned how. She always said she was too nervous to drive.

I will never forget the day we finally arrived at the Hood River camp. As we drove down the dirt road to the shelters, Paw kept beepin' the horn, announcin' to everyone that we was comin'. I could feel my heart poundin' with excitement. The Musgroves, Sawyers, and all the other families hurried to the field where everyone parked their cars. They were expectin' us 'cause Mr. Johnson told them that he got our card. Maw and Paw pulled in and got out of the car and began huggin' our friends. When me and Tim opened the back door of the car and got out, everyone started fussin' over us and sayin' how much we had changed. They said how grown-up we looked, 'specially me. 'Twas true. In two years, I had grown several inches and, accordin' to Maw, was lookin' more and more like a young woman. After all the hugs and hellos, I couldn't wait another minute and asked Mrs. Musgrove where Ben was. She said that she was purty sure he was out under the pines. Without sayin' another word, I took off walkin', then, when I got a good distance from everyone, started runnin' fast as I could. When I got to the pines and laid eyes on Ben down by the creek, I could feel my heart start a-poundin' again.

"Ben!" I said just loud enough for him to hear and yet tryin' not to sound too thrilled at seein' him.

He stood, turned, and then looked up at me and smiled. When our eyes met one another's, I coulda sweared my heart was doin' somersaults. Ben looked older. He was taller and broader now, and the hard work he'd been doin' the past two years showed. He looked so handsome that it started me frettin' and prayin' that he would think that I had changed for the better myself. The night before, we had stopped and camped on the Columbia like before to rest and clean up. Maw, knowin'—because I told her after that first summer at Hood River—how I felt 'bout Ben, rag tied my hair so as it would be full and pretty as could be for the next day. I even changed into my best Sunday dress, tryin' to be as presentable to Ben as I could.

"Hi. Whatcha doin'?" It was a cockamamy thing to say, but that was the only thing I could think o' sayin' at that moment. All's I had done for two years was think about him day and night, and now that I finally got to see him, all's I could say was "Whatcha doin'?"

"Nothin'," he said. "Just gettin' away by myself for a spell."

First thing I noticed was his voice. It had changed and was much deeper now. 'Nother thing I noticed right off was that he had grown an Adam's apple just like Paw's.

"You look . . ." I wanted to say "handsomer than anythin'," but that woulda been too bold so soon on, so I said, ". . . you look good."

Ben smiled and said, "You look . . ." and I could see his eyes drop to my chest speedy like, then jump back to my eyes. I could also see his face was goin' a bit pink, and then he paused for a moment and adjusted what he was intendin' to say. Finally he said, "You look real good too."

I knew exactly what he was hintin' 'cause Maw said I had gone from cherries to peaches in one season.

Neither one of us knew quite what to say after that, 'cept what a nice day it was, not too hot, not too cool. I started down the bank to where Ben was, and that's when it happened. I slipped on a rock, and my feet come right out from under me. I screamed and, to keep from fallin', began wavin' my arms every which way, tryin' my best not to lose my balance and fall. Next thing I know I'm in Ben's arms, lookin' up into his eyes. I wanted to kiss him or be kissed right there and then and got the notion that Ben might've felt the same. And then just when I thought it was about to happen, the big, flat rock we was standin' on started rockin' back and forth, causin' me and Ben to lose our evenness. He let go of me, and the two of us started swirlin' our arms, leanin' this a way and that, bendin' every which way to right ourselves. If someone happened along just then, they woulda thought we was doin' some kinda crazy, weird dancin'. Next thing we knew, we were falling right into the creek. Under the water we went with a big splash.

As fast as we went under, we came up out of the water. When we set eyes on one 'nother, we couldn't help but start laughin'. I laughed so hard it hurt my sides. I hadn't laughed that hard since last time I was with Ben.

Eleven

A SHORT SEASON

THAT SEASON, 'TWAS LIKE A DOUBLE-EDGED SWORD. ON the one hand, the sun did not seem so blazin' hot like other years, and the buckets seemed to be lighter and the ladder shorter, but on the other hand, to my great sadness, time seemed to pass ever so quickly. Each day, I dreaded that soon all the cherries would be picked and gone and we would be a-gettin' and a-goin'.

Ben and me made sure we spent nearly all of our time together. Even when we worked, Ben would place his ladder and pick in the tree next to where I was pickin'. We talked, teased, dallied, and laughed, and had contests to see who could pick the fastest and the most. Course, hard as I tried, never could I keep pace with Ben.

As happy as I was bein' with Ben 'most every minute of the day, somethin' began troublin' me. Not ever once did Ben make mention of how he was feelin' 'bout me, which got me to wonderin' if mebby he only thought of me as a friend or mebby a sidekick or just a pal to do things with like fish and swim and whatnot. These sorta thoughts began to torment me and busy all my attention. Each and every day, I hoped that mebby he would say somethin', anythin' to give me hope and ease.

'Bout a week before we figured we'd be leavin' Hood River and 'most probably goin' to Florida to pick citrus, I was sufferin' from a serious stretch of feelin' sorry for myself. I still didn't know where things stood 'tween me and Ben, and it was takin' its effect on me. S'pose I coulda come right out and asked him, "Do you love me like I love you?" But I couldn't do that, 'cause what if he didn't feel same as I did? Besides, Maw says it should be the boy who shares his feelin' first. "It is a man's duty, always was and still is," she said. I asked her why, and she just said, "That's just the way it is, darlin'—plain and simple. Trust me."

Maw told me that when she prays, she always prays that I will find someone who loves me more than hisself. Seems if you love someone more than yourself, it would be harder than anythin' to keep from tellin' 'em. To my way of thinkin', if Ben cared for me more than hisself, he woulda told me so. My head began achin' with the thought of it all. I thought bein' in love was s'posed to make you happy and joyful. *Mebby I'm just dreamin'.* I thought to myself. *Mebby I'm just a scatty girl with a cock-eyed, foolish notion that Ben loves me.* Bein' thought of by Ben as just a friend started a slow-burnin' anger smolderin' inside me. I refused to talk to Ben that day. He wasn't deservin' of me talkin' to him, in my mind. When I worked, it was with my back to him, and whenever he spoke to me, I pretended not to hear. I picked cherries with an awful vengeance. Each cherry picked was, in my way of thinkin', stickin' a dagger into Ben's heart for not carin' 'bout me as much as I cared 'bout him. I was up and down the ladder more that day than ever before, so much so that when we stopped for lunch, Paw asked, "What's gotten into you, girl?"

"Just feelin' like workin'," I said.

Maw knew what it was that was annoyin' me so. She knew 'cause I told her how I was feelin'. She told me to be patient and unhurried, and if things were s'posed to be, all would turn out. But how could I be patient and unhurried when we was leavin' in 'bout a week's time? Whenever Ben came near me that day, I found other things to busy myself. Even went to the outhouse and stared out through the cracks till Ben went back to work. I began to convince myself that I no longer loved Ben and that I could not wait another day to get on the road again. I started thinkin' that I should never have come back to Hood River. Worse than that, I never wanted to come back again.

Back up the ladder I went and hid myself from Ben inside the branches, where I began pickin'. But before long, I couldn't pick no more 'cause my true feelings for Ben were gettin' the better of my pretended feelings. My heart felt like it was gonna break. I grabbed hold of some branches, bowed my head, and sobbed openly but quietly so as Ben couldn't hear me in the next tree. Suddenly my ladder began shakin'. First thought was that the earth was quakin' or that mebby Mount Hood had made up her mind to start eruptin' again. Then I looked down, and to my surprise, Ben was makin' his way up my ladder! Quick as I could, I began wipin' my tears away so's he wouldn't know that I had been cryin'. Before I knew it, Ben was side by side with me on the ladder, wearin' a big, friendly smile.

"You okay?" he asked. "You've been actin' different all day. Is somethin' the matter? You feelin' sick?"

"No," I fibbed, "just feelin' like workin'. Soon we'll be leavin', and I'm just wantin' to make as much as I can for Maw and Paw, that's all."

Then Ben noticed my tears. "You been cryin'?"

"No," I said, "just somethin' irritatin' my eyes, is all."

The ladder was so narrow that Ben and me were just as close as we was the day at the creek. Bein' so close like this and lookin' into Ben's dark brown eyes caused me to take hold of a tree limb 'cause I was startin' to feel weak in the knees.

"I brought you somethin'." And then he fished somethin' from his shirt pocket, held it out, and showed it to me.

"Twin cherries" is what we migrants called them. It was two cherries attached to the same stem. 'Twas uncommon to find such as this, and when one did, it was most likely by accident. With his right hand, Ben ran his fingers up the side of my cheek and then brushed the hair away from my ear and carefully looped the cherries over it. He looked me directly in the eyes, and I could feel a warm flush spreadin' over my face and with it a washin' away of all the hateful and spiteful thoughts I'd had of him that day. But then I put a stop to that at short notice. I had no aim to be pals with Ben or anythin' in resemblance. I fixed my best pretended smile and said, "Thank you. Now I better get back to workin'."

I turned away from him and started pickin', pretendin' like Ben wasn't next to me on the same ladder. Then Ben did somethin' I wasn't 'spectin'. He put his hands on my shoulders and turned me so we was facin' each other again. I still remember wishin', hopin', and prayin' that he couldn't hear my heart a-poundin'. It was poundin' so loud I was sure he could. From there, things got even more disturbin'. He dropped his hands to my waist, scooped me up in his strong arms, pulled me in real close, and kissed me softly on the lips. After kissin' me, he pulled away, leavin' me dazed, with my eyes still closed and my lips still puckerin'. When I did open my eyes, he was smilin' at me. I felt foolish, flustered, and tongue-tied. But Ben didn't seem to mind, 'cause he leaned in to kiss me again. That was when we heard Tim shoutin' up from the ground, "Hey, what's goin' on up there?"

It scared us so bad we 'bout fell off the ladder.

For the rest of the day, I steered right clear of Ben. Once more my thoughts started gettin' the best of me. Who did Ben think he was, bein' so smart-alecky and bold, kissin' me the way he did? To my way of thinkin', a girl should never let a boy kiss her 'less she knows his intentions are right and proper. What were Ben's intentions? Did he even like me, or was he thinkin' I was some floozy girl willin' to give away my precious kisses just for the askin' or takin'? I promised myself I wasn't goin' to let that happen 'gain.

twelve

CONFESSIN'

THAT NIGHT, AFTER SUPPER, AS IT WAS OUR HABIT, THE migrants sat 'round the fire tellin' amusin' stories and singin' hymns. I was settin' with Maw and Paw and Tim, 'cross the fire from Ben and his folks. I tried my darndest not to look at him, but when I did, I noticed he was havin' a good time laughin' at all the stories. The more he laughed, the more agitated I was becomin'. How could he be enjoyin' hisself so when I was sufferin' like I was? Sick and tired out of the whole particular, I got up, left the fire, and wandered out to the pines.

'Twas a beautiful night, with a cloudless sky and a big, fat moon up above, lookin' like it was 'bout to burst. When I had got to the pines, it looked like someone had knocked over a giant pitcher of golden light, sendin' it crashin' and splashin' down through the trees, leavin' little puddles of light scattered all over the ground. Only thing that was missin' was Ben.

Little did I know that Ben was there, hidin' and watchin' me. When I had gotten up from the fire, Ben 'scused himself from the rest and then, lickety-split, hightailed it the long ways out to the pines.

When I got to the edge of the creek, I took off my shoes and dangled my feet in the cool water. After a little while, I heard somethin' in the bushes behind me. At the time I didn't know it was Ben throwin' sticks and stones in my direction, and it was startin' to scare the livin' daylights outta me.

Quick as I could, I put my shoes back on, wet feet and all, and started runnin' for the shelters fast as I could, when all at once Ben stepped from behind a tree and grabbed me! I screamed to high heaven, and Ben started laughin', thinkin' this was the funniest thing ever. I tried to get away, but Ben had my arms roped in by my sides.

"You 'bout scared me to death," I said.

"Why have you been stayin' away and ignorin' me all day?" Ben asked.

I lied and said, "I haven't been stayin' away."

"Then what'd you call it?"

"Just let go of me." I said it as mean soundin' as I could but not really meanin' nothin' by it.

Ben just stood there lookin' into my eyes for a moment, seemin' confused and somewhat hurt by the way I was actin'. Thinkin' back now, he musta been wonderin' why I was now actin' like I didn't like him when just that day I had let him kiss me.

Then he did somethin' that baffled me. He just let go of me, turned his back to me, and started walkin' away toward the shelters.

What had I done? I was afraid I had ruined everythin'. What if he did like me and now had his mind changed 'cause I was actin' like such a dickens. I couldn't let him walk off like that without him knowin' what I was really feelin'. But how was I s'posed to do that and not ruin it all? I was desperate.

"Ben," I called.

But he kept on a-goin'.

"Ben!" I shouted. "Come back here! You got some 'splainin' to do."

Ben stopped, turned, and started walkin' back to me. "What're you talkin' 'bout?"

My mind was racin', tryin' to think what to say next.

He looked down into my eyes. "What are you sayin'?" he demanded.

I was so nervous, it took me a space before I could spit it out. Finally, after takin' a deep breath, I said, "Today, in the tree. You kissed me—"

Then before I could say 'nother word, he did somethin' that left me muddled. He grabbed me, pulled me in real close, and kissed me before I could finish what I was sayin'.

"Like that?" he said, holdin' me out and away from him.

"Maw says—"

He kissed me again.

I pushed away and asked, "Do you think highly of me?"

This seemed to confuse Ben. "What do you mean?" he asked.

"Maw says a young man has no right to kiss a girl before confessin' his sincere affection for her."

Ben thought this over for a space, then said, "Ain't a kiss a way of confessin' all that? Least that's what my paw says."

"A kiss is only half a confession," I said.

Ben looked at me for the longest time before speakin'. "Well, whataya want me ta say?"

"What you feel . . . 'bout me."

"You tell first, then I'll tell."

"Nope," I said, shakin' my head. "Maw says it's the boy's duty to say first."

Ben rolled his eyes. "Seems your maw's got a lot to say, don't she?"

I just nodded and waited for Ben's answer.

"Let's see," he said, leanin' 'gainst a tree and scratchin' his head. "I must like you 'cause I'm hatin' that you is leavin' so soon and I won't see you mebby for 'nother year. Is that good enough for the other half of a confession?"

This was gettin' all too excitin'. Since things was kinda goin' in my favor, I thought I'd keep askin' more questions. At the time it seemed like the natural thing to do.

"Why do you like me?"

Ben smiled at me and shook his head 'mused like. "Cause you're fun."

"You're fun too," I said, smilin'.

Sayin' what I said musta gave Ben confidence to keep on confessin'.

"I know that I would never want to hurt you for nothin'."

"What else?" I asked, not rememberin' when I was havin' this much fun.

"When I see you in the mornin', it makes me smile."

When he said that, I couldn't help but break out into a big smile.

"Do you think I'm purty?" Yes, it was a bold thing to ask. But at the moment, it seemed like the forthright thing to say. It was like all the road blocks was taken away and we could say anythin' we wanted without worryin'.

"Yes, I think you are the purtiest girl with the purtiest eyes and purtiest smile I have ever seen."

I can tell you my heart was a-singin'. But a girl can't get 'nough of a good thing, so I pressed on and said, "Maw says she prays that I will find someone that loves me more than hisself."

"What's that s'posed to mean?" Ben asked, laughin'.

What I said next was somethin' I came up with while pickin' cherries that day.

"Well, what if," I said, "we was both in the North Pole, and we was freezin' to death, and we only had one blanket. What would you do with the blanket?"

At first Ben was grinnin' from ear to ear and shakin' his head, but as he looked at me and started 'maginin' what I had said, his smile slowly faded away, and seemed he began to turn all serious. Finally he said, "I would put it 'round you and keep you warm till I died."

After he said that, I didn't need no more confessin' from him. I moved close to him, put my arms 'round him, and rested my head on his chest. We just stood for a long time under that big, bright, jealous moon just holdin' on to each other.

Thirteen

NEW HOPE

THE NIGHT BEFORE WE WAS LEAVIN' HOOD RIVER FOUND ME and Ben under the pines again. We was kissin' when I suddenly broke away from him and started runnin'.

"Sal!" he called. "What's the matter?"

But I didn't answer. I ran across that big field and into the shelter. Maw and Paw were settin' in the chairs, and Tim was layin' on our bed, the one me and him shared. Cryin', I threw myself on Maw's bed and buried my head in the pillow.

"What's the matter?" Maw asked with concern.

"Nothin'," I sobbed.

"Yes, there is," said Maw patiently.

"No, nothin'!" I said strongly.

For a spell, there was silence, with just my sobbin' fillin' the room.

After a space, Maw said, "Care to talk about it, darlin'?"

"No. I would be ashamed to talk of what's troublin' me," I said.

"I think you would feel better if you talked a little." Maw's voice was filled with understandin' and love.

"All right," I said, turnin' toward her. "Tonight, out there, under the big tree, Ben and me was kissin'. Then I ran from him. Ran! Do you hear? And why? I'll tell you why. 'Cause I didn't trust him no more. I didn't trust myself. So I ran away. How do I know he won't get tired of waitin' for me? How do I know they'll be here next year? Or how do I know we'll be here? Mebby they or us will go over the side of a mountain, with bad brakes or icy roads. How do I know he'll wait and wait year after year? Forgive me for sayin' it, but I'd marry him right now if I could. Then he would be mine, and I would be his. I love him! Do you understand that?"

Goin' to Maw, I knelt at her feet with my head in her lap. "Oh, Maw and Paw, I do love him so much, and it just seems like a year is so far away."

No one spoke for a space, as Maw ran her fingers through my hair till I quieted down.

"There, now," Maw said. "Don't you feel better now that you have talked about it? Don't you know you can talk to us 'bout anythin'? All young people have the same trouble, settled or not."

Paw spoke for the first time. "We can thank God our young'uns can talk to us and tell us their troubles."

Kneelin' there at Maw's feet, I thanked God from the bottom of my heart for my maw and paw . . . thanked Him 'cause they was so understandin'.

Then Paw said somethin' that lifted my dampened spirits and gave me somethin' to cling to and hope for. "If you still want to marry Ben next year this time, and his folks are willin', we'll see to it you get married."

"Oh, Paw," I said, runnin' to him and throwin' my arms 'round his neck. Do you really mean it?"

"Course I do, darlin'," he said, holdin' me in his arms like he used to when I was just a young girl.

Paw wasted no time gettin' Ben and his folks to our shelter so we could figure some things before we left in the mornin'. Ben and me sat on the bed holdin' hands and listenin' to Paw. Paw said he wished we would wait longer, least till I was eighteen, but he said if next year, when we returned, if we still felt the same 'bout each other and felt we couldn't wait no longer, he would grant his permission for me to get married.

Then Paw looked at Ben's folks and said, "If you good folks are willin', we'll see to it they have a weddin' right here in Hood River."

I squeezed Ben's hand extra tight and looked to Ben's folks. Tears of happiness filled Ben's maw's eyes. She and Mr. Musgrove shared a look, then turned back to the rest of us, smiled, and nodded. Everyone let out a cheer and then hugged each other all around.

The next mornin', when Ben held me and kissed me good-bye, all my fears was washed away. I knew he would wait for me, and I for him. I knew that in a year, we would again meet under that big, friendly tree in the clearin' with the stream runnin' along one side and snowcapped Mount Hood piercin' the sky at the end of the long valley.

As we left camp and drove down the long dirt road to the highway, Ben ran alongside the car, wavin' and laughin'. I hung out the window so far that Tim had to hold on to me so as I wouldn't fall out. I waved, cried, and laughed till we couldn't see Ben no more.

As we set out that day, it was a blessin' and a tender mercy from the good Lord to keep us from knowin' the terrible tragedy, sorrow, and heartache the afterward months would bring.

Fourteen

BITTER WINTER

IT WAS EARLY OCTOBER. WE WAS PASSIN' THROUGH SOUTH-ern Illinois, close to St. Louis, when Maw took sick. I had never known her to be this sick.

We stopped at a doctor's place in a small town close to St. Louis and found out that her heart was very bad. The doctor was a cantankerous little old man with a stabile scowl on his face. Me and Tim sat against the wall as Maw unbuttoned her dress so as the doctor could listen to her heart with an instrument. When he heard what he needed to hear, he told Maw she could button up. Then he looked over his bifocals at Paw and said, "What was it you said you did, mister?"

"In these parts, we're called migrants."

The doctor studied Paw for a long moment, then spoke, "Fruit pickers." Then he motioned to Maw. "Does the missus pick with you?"

"She does," answered Paw.

"Well, let me tell you somethin', sonny. Unless you keep her off those darned ladders, you're gonna be pickin' alone. Do I make myself clear? Can't remember when I've heard a heart that sounded that bad."

Paw and Maw shared a worried look.

The doctor crossed to an old rolltop desk and began fillin' out a prescription.

"You can get this filled down at the corner," he said, handin' Paw the piece of paper.

"If I scared you," he continued, "I meant to. It's not good. It's bad. Worse than bad. You've got to be very careful with her. Any excitement or agitation of any kind could kill her."

When he said that, it took the breath right out of me, and I started to cry. Tim, I know, was feelin' same as me but, tryin' to be brave, reached over and gave me a comfortin' squeeze on the arm.

The doctor looked at Maw, then back at Paw. "Keep her quiet, make things easy for her. Understand?"

Then he scowled at me and Tim. "You kids are gonna have to fend for yourselves for a while. Understand? Your mother's gonna need all the help and rest she can get."

When he was through with us, he turned back to Paw. "Get her to a doctor soon as you get where you're goin'."

Paw got the pills from the corner drugstore, then we drove slowly out of town, with Maw lyin' in the back and Tim and me up front with Paw.

At the first chance he had, Paw talked to Tim. "We gotta settle, son. It won't be easy to find a job in this part of the country, as I'm gettin' older. These farmers won't hire me, and you're too young. But we gotta get somethin' somehow."

I turned away from Tim and Paw, leaned my forehead against the cold window, and stared out. A dull, sick, awful feelin' washed over me. The thought of losin' Maw was more than I could bear. Not to mention maybe never seein' Ben again. I wanted to talk to him, tell him about Maw, but how could I? There was no way of tellin' where he and his folks were. I closed my eyes and prayed that Maw would be okay and that things would work out for the best.

The past season had been a good one financially. The crops were good, the pay was good. We had, therefore, saved a little money—not much, but more than usual. We rented a small house that had a stove and one bed. Tim and I slept on the floor. It wasn't much, but it gave us a chance to look fer work. We answered several ads, but Paw was so old and Tim so young the farmers didn't want to or couldn't hire them.

Three or four days later, Paw met a farmer named Roberts who was lookin' for a hired hand. "Looky here," said Paw, "you say you need a man? Now, I know I'm no good to you, but my son here is a top hand, even if he is young. I know mebby you can't hire him outright, but you can hire me, and you can work him. You see, we was a-goin' to my younger brother's, but my wife took sick. We gotta hang around a spell for her to get on her feet again. You might try us out. If we don't suit you, at least you can use us till you find someone you do want."

After thinkin' for a few moments, the farmer said, "Okay, we'll use you this winter—mostly chorin', anyhow. Come spring, we'll see how it works out."

Mr. Roberts wasn't really doin' us a favor, no more than he was doin' himself a favor. Workin' Tim that way, he could pay less money. Really, he was payin' us five dollars less than he would someone else. Still, it did give us a break, so no one complained.

Mr. Roberts had two farms, the one we lived on and

his where he lived, which was about one and a half miles from us. There was cattle where we lived, 'bout seventy head. At his place, there were both cattle and hogs.

'Twas Tim's job to do the chores at home, then go over and feed at Mr. Roberts's. Then he did any other jobs that came up, like fixin' fence, grindin' feed, or any other of the numerous things that come up on a farm. I did all the cookin' and helped with the milkin' and gatherin' eggs. Because our meat was furnished, along with eggs and milk, even with low pay, we could save a little.

'Twas a bad winter, with lots of snow, and very cold. We were lucky that there was a lot of timber on the place. What spare time Tim had, he and Paw worked wood for fuel. Whenever I could, I helped, and I became quite good with an ax. Hard workin' helped that awful winter pass by a little quicker.

All's I could think about was marryin' Ben. I prayed and prayed that Maw would get better in time so we could go back to Hood River that summer. But Maw wasn't gettin' better. Seemed like she was gettin' worse.

And then one night it seemed my fortunes began lookin' brighter. We were all sittin' 'round the supper table eatin' our supper when Paw looked down the table at Maw and said, "Soon gonna be cherry pickin' time at Hood River."

"Wish we could go," said Tim.

"Maybe we oughta," said Paw.

I looked up at Paw and then at Maw, too afraid to say nothin' for fear of gettin' my hopes too high.

"Your Maw and I was talkin' last night 'bout what good kids we got. Your Maw's gettin' sick and tired of this here wallpaper. Says she needs a change of scenery.

Whataya think, kids? S'pose Maw could rest in the backseat of the car just as well as she can in that rockin' chair?"

I couldn't believe what I was hearin'. I looked at Maw, who smiled back at me and gave me a wink.

I was ready to burst with excitement. "You ain't foolin', are ya, Paw? Do you really mean it?"

"S'pose we could get you up to Hood River and married," said Paw, "and git ourselves back here in two weeks?"

Tim broke into a big smile. "Can't see why not, Paw."

I could feel the tears wellin' up in my eyes. All's I could say was, "I love you, Paw. I love you, Maw."

"S'pose if Mr. Roberts says it's okay, we oughta be a-gettin' and a-goin' come first of July."

I jumped up from the table, ran to Paw, and threw my arms 'round him, then ran to Maw and threw my arms around her.

I was so happy and excited I could hardly sleep that night. I had saved the twin cherries Ben gave to me that day in the tree. Course all that was left was the two cherry pits. Each night I would take them out of my drawer, hold them tight, and make a wish. Seemed like it was workin' 'cause Maw and Paw was helpin' that wish come true.

I guess Mr. Roberts liked how Paw and Tim was runnin' things 'cause he said Paw and Tim could keep on through the summer. He had a man who could handle things for the two weeks while we was gone to Oregon. We'd be leavin' right 'round the first week in July so as to be in Hood River just before pickin' time. Never was there a happier girl. I was dancin' on air till that one, terrible, fateful day.

Fifteen

CALLED TO AN EARLY HARVEST

LONG 'BOUT FIVE THIRTY IN THE AFTERNOON ONE DAY toward the end of February, I was gettin' supper. Maw was settin' in the front room in a rocker, facin' the kitchen, and could see the kitchen door from where she sat. Workin' over the stove, I could see the barn through the deepenin' dusk.

Paw came through the kitchen, pausin' to kiss Maw, sayin', "I'll go start feedin' the cattle so Tim won't have so much to do."

Every evenin' he did the same thing, and I thought nothin' of it at the time.

Close to six Tim drove up from Roberts's, and, like always, he went straight to the barn to feed. Usually he was finished 'bout six thirty, then we would eat and spend the evenin' together. As I saw him walkin' to the barn, I thought how lucky I was to have a brother so willin' to shoulder the responsibilities that he had, bein' only fifteen.

"Maw," I said, "can't remember when I have been this happy."

"I'm so happy for you, darlin'," she answered.

When I looked up from the stove and out the window,

I was shocked. The barn door swung open, and Tim was comin' toward the house, half carryin', half draggin' Paw through the snow. I could see right away that Tim was cryin' and Paw was bleedin' from the mouth onto his shirt and holdin' his side. His face was all twisted with pain. Horrified, I forgot everythin' and called out, "Paw!" Then I ran outside, forgettin' 'bout Maw sittin' there where she could see us. Runnin' to Paw, I got his arm over my shoulder, and Tim and I carried him along through the snow and the mud.

"What happened?" I cried.

"Paw fell out of the haymow where the floor is broken and landed on the stall gate," Tim sobbed in reply.

Somehow we got Paw up onto the back porch and through the kitchen door. When we dragged Paw inside, Maw saw us right off, and when she did, she threw both hands over her mouth and cried out, "Paw!"

Then she jumped up from the rocker and started movin' toward the kitchen, when all of a sudden, she grabbed her chest, went down on her knees, then fell to the floor without makin' another sound.

"Oh, my!" said Tim frantically. "Get Maw. I'll help Paw to the bed."

"No, son," Paw said, gaspin' for every painful breath. "Help me get to my darlin'."

I had already left Paw, runnin' to Maw. I tried to get her up but couldn't. She just fell back, so I cradled her in my arms, rockin' her back and forth. Then Tim let Paw down by Maw. Paw's hand feebly went to Maw's breast and felt for her heartbeat.

"Oh, dear God!" he cried. "You have taken her from me! You have taken her away!"

I was stunned. I sat on the floor, puttin' Maw's head in my lap. For the first time in my life, I saw Paw cry. And I cried with him.

Tim, pale with shock, got to his feet and backed toward the door. With a great effort, Paw stopped cryin'. "Son, come back." Paw's voice was weak, but Tim heard and stopped in midstride.

"Can't, Paw! Gotta get a doctor!" We had no phone, so Tim would have to drive to Roberts's.

"First, listen to me, or you will always regret it," said Paw. Then he coughed and tried to hide a trickle of blood from his mouth. "I don't have much time left, so listen close."

"Gotta go, Paw! Just gotta go!" said Tim as he started cryin'.

"Stop that!" said Paw, sternly as he could. "Stop right now. You don't have time for that now. Do you wanta lose Sal? Do you wanta be separated and sent to homes of some kind?"

"No, no, Paw!" Tim sobbed.

Just sayin' that little bit wearied Paw. He lay quietly for a few minutes, then he said slowly, "I'm busted inside. I know that. Now, if the law finds you kids are alone, they will send you to homes of some kind."

Through my tears, I could see the agony in Paw's eyes, though he was tryin' hard to keep us from knowin' the pain he was in.

"Can't help you much, my boy. And I know it's a man-sized job, but you take care of Sal, will you? Promise me, son." Paw's voice was fadin' and his breath weakenin'.

"Don't you worry, Paw—I'll take care of Sal," promised Tim with tears floodin' his eyes and streamin' down his cheeks. "Somehow . . . somehow, I'll find the Musgroves or the Sawyers, and they'll help."

"Good boy, son. Now, go get the doctor," said Paw. As Tim went out again, Paw coughed and wiped the blood on the pillowcase that Tim had put under his head.

"Sal," Paw said faintly.

"Yes, Paw," I sobbed as I reached over and took his hand.

"Stop cryin', darlin'," said Paw. "You gotta think. Gotta help Tim what you can." Again he coughed, and again that trickle of blood. His eyes closed. I held his hand, a hand that grew cooler as the minutes passed. With his other hand, he cradled Maw's hand.

Tim went to the boss's house fast as he could and told them to get a doctor and then left without waitin' for an answer. As he came in, Paw opened his eyes. Oh, the pain was so plain in his face. Together, the three of us crouched on the floor, waitin'.

The doctor got there quickly, although it seemed like ages. The boss was with him. As they came in and looked at us on the floor, the boss asked, "What happened?"

Paw looked up and gasped, "Fell from the barn . . . I know I'm all busted inside."

The doctor knelt on the floor next to Paw and felt his pulse. Shakin' his head, he got up and went to his bag. When he came back, he gave Paw a shot, for pain. Then, standin' up, he told the boss that, no matter what, we don't dare move him. The pain pill seemed to do Paw some good 'cause he slept for mebby half an hour after. When he opened his eyes again, he reached for me and Tim, took us both by the hand, and looked deep into our eyes. He couldn't speak 'cause of the terrible pain he was in, but he didn't have to speak. I knew what he was sayin'. He was sayin', "I love you. Oh, how I love you! I'm awful sorry that I gotta be a-gettin' and a-goin.' I know you're just young'uns, but don't worry, the good Lord will be watchin' out for you. Be good to each other, and by and by we'll all be together again soon." And then, lettin' go of Tim, he took hold of Maw's hand and closed his eyes for the very last time.

Just before midnight, the funeral parlor people came and took Maw and Paw away together. Next day, the local paper stated Paw and Maw died three hours apart.

The boss and his wife tried to get us to go to their house, almost insistin' on it, till Tim looked at them through tears and with a tremblin' chin and said, "Can't you please see we want to be alone? Won't you please leave us be for a little bit?"

I added, "Please leave us. We'll be all right." Those were almost the only words I can remember sayin' after Paw died.

With genuine sympathy, they went to the door and said, "If you need anythin', anythin' at all, let us know, will you?" We only nodded our heads as they left.

As soon as they were gone, Tim and I silently walked side by side into Maw and Paw's bedroom. We laid across the bed and lost ourselves in tears.

I don't know how long we lay there, don't know how long we cried, but when we did stop, we was all dry inside—empty, alone, afraid.

The neighbors we had met and were friendly with while we'd been at Roberts's were now people to fear. Oh, the questions! Paw or Maw always had the answers, now what was we gonna say?

One time Paw had said to never think of an answer in advance. Each person, each group, has to be handled different. Each answer has to fit the person or persons accordin' to the situation.

Finally Tim spoke in the darkness. "We gotta stop this. Paw would be ashamed of us. And tomorrow we gotta face people, gotta look them in the eye and have all the answers."

"Let's pray, Tim," I suggested, rememberin' with pain the many times Maw had said the same words.

Kneelin' beside Maw and Paw's bed, we prayed for strength and asked God to help us find our kind. We didn't know how much harder we would be a-prayin' and what this new life had in mind for us. 'Twas a good thing God in mercy didn't reveal that to us.

Since we'd lived here, Tim and I'd been sleepin' alone, but not tonight—the rest of this night we lay on Maw and Paw's bed, tryin' to find comfort from each other. Yes, we lay there, but neither of us slept. Sometimes I cried, sometimes Tim did, and in our helplessness, we tried to comfort each other.

That long, long night finally came to an end as gray dawn began to show itself through the window.

"Gotta get up," Tim said heavily. "Soon people will be a-comin', and we gotta look like somethin'—gotta make everyone believe everythin' will work out."

We dragged ourselves down the stairs and into the kitchen. Washin' our faces in cold water and combin' our hair, we looked some better, but our eyes were red-rimmed and heavy-lidded. Neither of us felt like eatin', so we drank coffee in silence, each with our own thoughts and fears.

After coffee, Tim went out and did the feedin' while

I tidied up the house, 'cause nothin' had been done the night before. The food still sat in the kettles and pans. The dishes, 'cludin' Maw and Paw's, was still on the table. Not that I felt like cleanin' up and all—or that Tim felt like doin' chores, but we couldn't have people comin' here thinkin' we couldn't take care of ourselves.

Somehow, we had to be left alone. Somehow we had to get away from here. We couldn't have people holdin' us up so long that they learned 'bout us. Nope, it had to be done just right. We had to get away soon as the funeral was over. Heaven knows Tim ain't old enough to drive. And I wasn't either. And as fate would have it, this was the first year that everyone had to have a driver's license. However, there wasn't much to it. They only cost a quarter. Still, you had to be old enough to get one 'fore you could drive legally. Tim could drive. He'd driven some, back and forth from Mr. Roberts's place. But any other time, Paw was always settin' by him. Somehow, someway, we had to get outta here. No one would let us drive away if they knew what we was about. Thoughts chased through my mind like scutterin' rabbits, always comin' back to somehow, someway, we gotta get away.

About eight o'clock, the boss came over. Tim was in the house by then. When we let Mr. Roberts in, he said to Tim, "Saw you did the chores here. Didn't need to do that."

"We're still livin' in your house," said Tim.

"We didn't expect you to," said Mr. Roberts kindly. "Gotta talk to you, Tim," said Mr. Roberts. "You're only a boy and . . ."

Tim cut him off real quick, knowin' where he was goin', and said, "You don't need to worry 'bout us, Mr.

Roberts. I called Uncle Jim last night after you left."

"You did?" said Mr. Roberts, surprised.

Now I'm a-thinkin', I ain't never heard of no Uncle Jim.

"Yes, sir," said Tim. "I went into town and used the pay phone."

"Will he be here for the funeral?" asked Mr. Roberts.

"Afraid not. He couldn't start right out, and it's a long way," said Tim, lookin' Mr. Roberts right in the eye, soundin' so sincere, just the way Paw had done so many times.

"Where's he comin' from?" asked Mr. Roberts.

"Don't you remember? Paw told you. Oregon," Tim replied confidently.

"Oh, yes—yes, I do remember now," said Mr. Roberts.

My insides were churnin'. I was so nervous I could hardly sit still. Tim was still talkin', conversin'. He's lookin' right at the boss like he should, but I knew he was scared. I wasn't used to Tim handlin' things, not quite sure he knew how, but seemed he was doin' a pretty good job of it. I felt like goin' and hidin' like a scared pup but couldn't do that. I needed to know what's bein' said just in case the same question was asked of me when Tim wasn't 'round.

"The missus and I have been talkin'," said Mr. Roberts, "Maybe it would be better for you kids to come stay with us. 'Tain't right, you kids stayin' here alone."

"Mr. Roberts," Tim said, "Sal and I have been handlin' things a long spell now. You've seen us doin' it, and we'll do okay now. But we sure do want to thank you."

"'Tain't that," said Mr. Roberts. "It's not that you can't handle things. It's just that you're both so young."

"But old enough to do your work," Tim answered. "I ain't askin' you to keep me as a hired hand. I'm only askin' to stay in your house till our uncle gets here. If he don't get here the day of the funeral, he'll be here the next day for sure. Besides, I'll do the chores at this place as long as we're here. That'll pay our rent and save you comin' here twice a day."

"Well, all right," replied Mr. Roberts slowly. "You can stay here till the day after the funeral. Then, if your uncle isn't here by then, you'll hafta come to our house till he does come."

"Thank you, sir. That's all we ask. We just wanta be alone till uncle Jim gets here," said Tim.

Mebby Mr. Roberts wouldn't have left us alone even then, but he had quite a houseful as it was. They had two teenagers, and his wife's sister was there livin' with them, and she had a baby in arms.

One thing I'll say for Mr. Roberts, he meant the best. He had proven to be a good man to work for. 'Sides that, he had agreed to handle the preparations for the funeral, and we didn't know from nothin' about those things. Also, he was goin' to pay half the expenses. I suppose 'cause Paw was killed in his barn. Then, too, Tim was young, and mebby he was afraid our uncle would raise some Cain because he was workin' Tim. Or could be he just felt sorry for us.

By ten o'clock, four women from the church were there. They had some hot soup and insisted on us eatin' it. All of them wanted us to go to their homes, but we just *had* to stay by ourselves so we could get away.

Mebby if we had told the truth, they would have helped us find our friends, but we couldn't take the chance. Most people look down on migrants, and the good people might have called the law to make sure we didn't go nowhere.

We didn't know till later, but that same day some of the church people were takin' up a collection to help with our expenses. All in all, we only had to pay forty-five dollars for the funeral.

I don't like to think of the day of the funeral. It was a pitiful thing. Of course, Tim and me were there with the boss and his wife and a very few from the church—nine people in all, not countin' the minister and the pallbearers. 'Twas a cloudy, cold day, to fit our spirits. On the way back from the graveyard, Tim asked the boss to stop at the Western Union. Soon as the boss stopped, Tim jumped out of the car and ran into the office. He stayed there just a short time, and as he came out, he had a Western Union telegram in his hand and was readin' it. As he got into the car, he put the telegram in his pocket and said, "Uncle Jim will be here tonight or early tomorrow mornin'. Aunt Clara is comin' with him. She's gonna drive our car back, I guess."

"That's nice," said Mr. Roberts. "Too bad he couldn't have got here today.

"He would have, if he could," Tim said, "but that must be a long drive."

I couldn't believe my ears. If I didn't know Tim, I woulda sweared he was tellin' the truth. My curiosity gettin' the best o' me, I reached over and took the telegram from Tim's shirt pocket 'fore he could stop me. I unfolded it and saw that it was blank. The Robertses didn't want to let us out at the house when we got there, but Tim and I insisted. We told them we'd likely see them before we ever left.

"In any case," Tim said, "we'll write to you now and then."

"You do that," said Mrs. Roberts. "We'll be so worried about you kids. You've been so good and all—so good to your mother and father. Oh, I'm so sorry! I shouldn't have said that." She was embarrassed. Then she said hurriedly, "You try and stop by at our house on your way out, will you?"

"Sure will," said Tim, openin' the door. "You people have been purty swell yourselves. Mebby we can get our uncle and Aunt Clara to stop for a little spell."

We both got out, and Tim closed the car door. We watched them slowly drive away.

After they had gone, we walked into the house and started gettin' ready to leave. Tim gathered all of our money up and, just like Paw, laid it on the table. I counted it like Maw would and after finishin' said, "Sixty-two bobs." Then, like Maw would say, I said, "That'll do all right." But I didn't believe myself when I said it.

We packed all our campin' equipment and put it in the car. We had it all figured. If the boss came over and said somethin', we'd just say we was gettin' ready in case our uncle should drive up. Then we went through the whole house, checkin' every room and drawer to make sure we left nothin' with names or places on it.

From then on, it was just the waitin'. We had to wait till everyone was in bed. But we couldn't wait too long, 'cause by daylight we had to be somewhere way out in the country.

Another worry Tim had was that he hadn't driven much, and never at night. When it got dark, Paw always made him stop and took over the wheel.

About chore time, the boss did come, but Tim had done the chores a little early. Lucky for us, it was already gettin' dark, which helped 'cause he didn't notice the car, as it was parked in the shadows.

Again the boss told us to try to get our uncle to stop and see him and his family before we left. We promised that we would, and he left.

We waited till ten thirty, then Tim lugged the big suitcase with all our clothes in it from the upstairs to the door. Then I emptied all the groceries from the cupboard into another suitcase. Soon as I closed the suitcase, Tim said, "Let's go."

We turned out the light, closed the door, and then hurried to the car and got in. We looked outta place sittin' there in the front seat, 'specially Tim, who could hardly see over the steerin' wheel. We looked at each other, worried like.

"First cop that sees me is gonna stop me. Huh?"

"Can you sit on somethin'?" I asked.

"If I do, I won't be able to reach the gas or the brakes."

Just then I saw somethin' on the seat next to Tim. It was Paw's hat. "Try this," I said.

I handed the hat to Tim, who held it for a moment, lookin' at it. I knew what he must be thinkin' 'cause I was thinkin' the same thing. I was missin' Paw and wishin' that he was here to take care of us.

Tim put on the hat. It was too big.

"Do I look older?"

"You look taller," I said.

Tim gripped the wheel and slipped in the key. He looked at me and, with a bit of tender emotion in his voice, said, "Be a good darlin' and pour a cup of coffee. Believe we could enjoy one right now."

Tim sittin' at the wheel and me sittin' in Maw's place

shook us all up again. We shoulda been in the backseat on top of all that stuff—not up here. Tim started the car, and we drove slowly away from the place of sadness, singin' "Draw Me Nearer."

Neither of us looked back.

Sixteen

THE ANSWER

THE SKY HAD CLEARED. THE MOON WAS A BIG, YELLOW DISK. The flat, snow-covered fields were shimmerin' in the moonlight. At first the traffic 'twasn't so bad. There wasn't many cars, and the highway wasn't in bad shape. But the closer we got to a city, the more cars we saw. Even at this time of night, there was a lot of traffic.

"Sal, help me watch for signs. I'm goin' crazy in all this traffic."

Tim was drivin' real slow and real careful, so many cars were passin' us, some honkin' impatiently as they whizzed by.

"Can you go any faster?" I asked.

"Can't!" Tim said. "I'm scared!"

Just then, comin' up from behind us, we could hear a siren. It was growin' louder and louder. I turned around and could see the cops comin', and I thought I would faint.

"Oh, no!" Tim said as he pulled off the highway onto a side road and stopped. "What'd I do wrong?"

The cops flew by us, clearly chasin' somebody else. Tim was grippin' the wheel so hard his knuckles were turnin' white.

Tim had hit rock bottom. "What're we gonna do, Sal?" he asked. "It just ain't gonna work. Might as well give up, tell everybody about what we are and who we are. We just can't do this without Maw and Paw."

The thought of Maw and Paw started us cryin' again. "I shoulda married Ben," I said. "Then we coulda gone anywhere we wanted. Wouldn'ta had to worry about the law or nothin'." As I was goin' on and on, Tim slowly raised his head off the wheel, wiped his tears away, and looked at me.

"That's it, Sal! You've got it!" he said all excited.

I didn't have the scantiest idea what he was talkin' about. "Got what?" I asked.

Tim was too worked up to answer. Without sayin' a thing, he opened the door and jumped out.

"Tim, where are you goin'?" I shouted and then jumped out myself and followed him to the rear of the car.

"Tim! Tell me what you're thinkin'?"

Still he didn't answer. His eyes were wild with excitement as he opened the trunk and shined his light inside.

"Tim, I shouted, what's goin' on in your head?"

He found a map, unfolded it, then looked up at me and declared, "Sal! We're gettin' married!"

"What?" I said, thinkin' maybe Tim had lost his mind.

Tim didn't answer. He was slidin' his finger 'cross the unfolded map and stoppin' right when he reached Little Rock, Arkansas.

"Do you remember William Clark?" he asked me, burstin' with excitement.

"Yeah. Why?"

"Remember how he and Ollie had to get married?"

"Yeah," I said, "but what's that gotta do with us?"

"Plenty. They was just 'bout our age, right? Mebby a year older."

"So?" I asked.

"So from here on out, I'm William Clark, and you, my sweet darlin', are gonna be Ollie Clark, with a 'Mrs.' on the front."

"Tim," I said, "I ain't sure what you're gettin' at."

"They got married in Little Rock, right?"

"I believe so," I said.

"So all's we gotta do is go to Little Rock and get us a duplicated marriage license."

"I see where you're goin', but how you gonna get it?"

Tim rubbed his chin, like Paw used to, actin' the part. "Mister," he said, "we was married here 'bout a year ago last summer. Our house burnt down, and we lost our license. We would 'preciate it if you would let us get a duplicate of it."

After he said this, he looked confidently at me with a twinkle in his eyes.

"Tim," I said, "it might work."

"It's gotta work. And 'nother thing," Tim said, "we gotta start drivin' just at night, stayin' off the highways and drivin' only on the secondary roads."

"That'll make it 'bout twice as far," I said, "but I s'pose it'll work."

Lookin' at the map again, Tim said, "No way out of it, we gotta go through the city of St. Louis."

He grabbed the map, folded it up, closed the trunk, and said, "C'mon, let's go."

Seventeen

LITTLE ROCK

WE HEADED SOUTH AND THEN STRAIGHT WEST TOWARD Glasgow, Missouri. Most of the roads we traveled wasn't even on the map, and we kept runnin' into one dead end after 'nother. One time, one road just plain ended into a pasture with a herd o' cattle caught in our headlights, starin' back at us like we was fools. Seemed we back-tracked as much as we went forward.

On the way to Glasgow, we got lost, and 'cause there was no way to turn south without goin' back, we decided to go west to Slatter, 'bout twenty-four miles west of Glasgow. 'Twas a long way 'cross there, 'cause we got a late start, so we never got to Glasgow before daylight.

Through this area, there was a lot of hills covered with trees of all kinds. The hills weren't big, but short and steep. Besides that, the towns were quite a ways apart—even the farmhouses weren't very close together. It was very poor farmland, but a lot of cattle ranged there.

At dawn we found a gravel road and wandered up and down the hills. At the foot of one of those hills, we found a narrow road goin' back into some timber. It looked just like a road some farmers might have used to carry wood out of. We followed this road for nearly a half a mile till we were sure we was outta sight. We were afraid to build a fire to cook on—scared someone would see it. There weren't no water there either, so when we got thirsty, we ate the snow that was on the ground.

Before we left the farm, we put two five-gallon cans of gas in the trunk. We emptied one of these into the car's gas tank. We really hadn't got very far 'cause of the slow rate of speed we was goin'. Lucky we had got out into the country before full daylight, but even then, we didn't feel safe. Anyone coulda come 'long and asked questions, mebby a farmer or a hunter, and heck, we couldn't give a good reason for settin' there all loaded that way.

We had lots of groceries, but no water or fire. I had packed a small lunch—just a couple of sandwiches, an apple each, and our thermos bottle of coffee—figurin' we could cook when we stopped. After we ate, we went to sleep. S'pose we musta been awful tired 'cause we didn't even get in the back but slept settin' up in the front seat, covered with a blanket.

We didn't sleep long, wakin', near as we could tell, 'bout noon. We was hungry and thirsty. Like I said, we was outta water, so we ate more snow. For breakfast, we each had a wiener sandwich and some coffee.

"Sal, you know what we're up against?" asked Tim.

"Guess so," I replied. "We're kids, alone, with no one to turn to."

"Worse than that," said Tim. "How we gonna buy gas? Can't just drive up like most people. What's the people gonna say when we drive in all loaded like this? Can't go to a farmer and ask for work like Paw used to. They would ask where we're runnin' from or to. They would say it's best we go home. 'Sides, there ain't no work on these kinds of farms, not this time of year, anyhow."

"We got this far, ain't we?" I said. "Let's worry 'bout the gas and where and how we're gonna get it when the time comes. For now, we got to get our sleep so we can stay awake while we're drivin' at night.

Finally we slept again—didn't sleep good nor long at a time. Seemed that we would doze off, then wake again. We both had a headache, s'pose from grievin', lack of sleep, lack of eatin', and too much strain on our nerves, not countin' lack of water.

Soon as it was dark, we drove out of there, followin' the gravel road till we came to a small town. It wasn't much, just a small country town. We drove into town, made a right-hand turn, and parked on a side street. Turnin' to me, Tim said, "Sal, we just gotta eat. And somehow we gotta get gas."

"Tim," I said, "let's buy supper tonight! I know we can't afford it, 'cause we gotta have money for gas. Tomorrow mebby we can try somethin' different."

The main street had a grocery store, drugstore, hardware store, restaurant, and clothin' store. On the far end of town, there was a fillin' station, a farm elevator, and an implement store.

As we went into the restaurant, a few farmers sittin' at the counter looked at us but again turned to their own eatin' and visitin'.

When the waitress brought the water, she asked, "Strangers hereabouts?"

Ignorin' her, Tim said, "Bring us coffee first, then a couple of hamburger steaks." As she served us, she never said another word.

Once back in the car, Tim said, "Can't act like that no more. Gotta answer their questions and be polite or people will have reason to believe somethin' is sure nuff wrong."

Takin' the gas cans from the trunk, we walked to the fillin' station. As the attendant filled the cans, he asked, "What's the matter? Your dad run out of gas?"

"Heck, no, mister, if Paw was drivin', he woulda watched it," said Tim as he winked at the attendant. "Maw was drivin'."

Laughin', the attendant said, "You gotta watch them women."

Just to get into the spirit of things, I said, "Yeah, but Paw drove it last."

Again the attendant laughed and asked, "Gotta carry it far?"

"Nope, just 'round the next corner," said Tim.

As we drove away, Tim said, "Well, that'll work so long as the money holds, but what we got won't hold long."

Now, I don't want you to think our sorrow was all washed away, but I suggested to Tim that we sing. That's what the folks woulda wanted.

So we sang. Our hearts weren't in it, but we did sing "The Old Rugged Cross" a couple of times. Then when we sang "Home Sweet Home," who is there that would blame us for havin' tears in our eyes and a catch in our voice now and then?

"Tomorrow I'll git out the old Bible," I said. "Will you read it, like Paw used to?"

"Sure I'll read it," said Tim. "We shoulda done it today instead of feelin' sorry for ourselves."

By next mornin', we were in the Ozark Mountains,

havin' made better time with no large cities to pass through and not as much traffic. This day was a little better. We had a place to hide without too much worry. We cooked open-pan biscuits and boiled taters and a can of green beans. We slept good. Tim was in the front seat while I was in the back. It was nearly dark before we woke up.

The big trouble right then was we had to drive to Little Rock in the daytime to get to the courthouse when it was open. Not wantin' to drive clear uptown, we parked on the outskirts, where the houses were still quite a ways apart. We found a side street or road that came to a dead end, with no houses 'cept one sittin' on quite a high bluff. The sides of the road were covered with trees. Not seein' any signs that said not to, we parked at the far end of the road. Then we had about a two-mile hike into town. At about nine thirty, we arrived at the courthouse.

We had no trouble gettin' the duplicate at all. Tim said his brother got married and lost the license, and since we was visitin' here, he wanted us to get it for him. Cost was one dollar.

Rememberin' our parts as we walked out, I put my arm through Tim's. Good thing, 'cause a policeman walked by just then. I looked at Tim, smilin' like we was truly in love. The officer gave us a knowin' look and big smile.

'Twas our plan to go move the car someplace so we could sleep, but just before we got to the car, we saw the highway patrol stoppin' all the cars and lookin' at their drivers licenses. They were close to where we was parked, so we turned 'round and walked back into town.

We walked up one street, down 'nother—just walkin' and winda shoppin' and actin' like a couple of lovers. I can tell you it ain't easy lookin' at your own brother and makin' people think you're in love like a young married couple.

We walked past a sweet shop and oh, how we wanted a malt, but we knew how far a dollar would go. Just two coffees and a burger would be 'most a dollar. We couldn't wait till we could cook. We walked till we was real tired. When we went back to the car, the highway patrol was still stoppin' cars and checkin' licenses, so we turned 'round and went back into town again. We felt we just had to rest, so we went into the bus depot. We was afraid to go sit down, case someone would ask us where we was goin' and mebby even ask to see our tickets. After walkin' in, we first got a drink. Lookin' over everybody, we saw a middle-aged man with a big suitcase, sittin' and readin' his paper. Sittin' beside him, we knew we looked, for all the world, like a little family waitin' for our bus. I couldn't help smilin' and wonderin' what that man woulda thought if he knew the part he was playin' in our lives. We sat there just a short time, even dozed off, till he went for his bus.

Not bein' able to stand it no longer, we finally bought two cups of coffee and a hamburger, which we shared. Wastin' as much time as we could, we went to the library— anywhere, everywhere, any place where we looked like we belonged. In a way it was kind of pleasant. This was the first time we'd been around people since we left Illinois, but oh, we were so tired, stayin' all day in town.

When night settled in, we walked back to our car. By this time, thank goodness, the highway patrol had gone. Not wantin' to waste another minute, we got right in the car and drove away.

Eighteen

NEW PLAN

AFTER LEAVIN' LITTLE ROCK, OUR PURPOSE WAS TO GO through Oklahoma, then the northwestern tip of Texas, and then into Arizona, hopin' to find someone there we knew.

Tim couldn't drive night and day like Paw could, so we stopped north of Little Rock, near the timbered hills of the Ozarks, where we found a place to hide and cook. Since we'd been up all day, we got to sleep some. And then we got a real good scare. As we was sleepin', two men pulled up next to us and stopped.

"Oh, Tim!" I said, all panicked inside but tryin' to act all normal on the outside, "What are we gonna do? What are we gonna say?"

The driver rolled down his window and motioned for Tim to do the same.

I could tell Tim was thinkin' awful hard. He just looked at me, then rolled the window down. "Howdy," he said all breezy like.

"What are you kids doin' way out here. Havin' troubles?"

"Naw," said Tim, all relaxed. "Just waitin' for our

Paw." And then Tim motioned toward a clump of trees down yonder in the gulch and chuckled. "He couldn't wait to get to the next town."

The two men looked at each other and smiled. "Okay," said the driver. "You kids have yourselves a fine day."

When they drove off, me and Tim looked at each other all scared like, with big eyes. Soon as we figured all was clear, Tim took the flashlight to find good dry wood. I went to the trunk to get dishes and kettles for cookin'. The trunk ain't had a lock since we had it, so I just opened it and felt inside with my hands. But I couldn't feel nothin'! I reached in further and still couldn't feel nothin'.

"Tim!' I shouted out. "Tim! Quick! Bring the light! Can't find nothin'!" Tim came runnin' and turned the flashlight into the trunk. Right off, we could see it was empty! Our spare was gone, car jack, tools, and dishes. We was cleaned out. Even our gas cans was gone. Nothin' left to eat. All we had left was what was in the part of the car that had been locked: blankets, a suitcase, and Paw's old, worn-out Bible.

Starin' for a long moment into the trunk, Tim finally said, "Shoot, dad gum, gotta start all over." The way he said it, I knew our cryin' days was over. We both knew that from now on, we would live each hour as it came like we was raised to do. No more would we be worryin' 'bout the next hour. We'd take each minute as it came from then on.

Oh, we knew what had happened, parkin' the car the way we had and walkin' the streets all day. We left it easy for someone.

"Nothin' to do now but drive on," said Tim. "Sure can't cook nothin', and we gotta eat."

"But, Tim," I said. "You need rest."

"Better to drive now while we can and find an all-night restaurant. We'll figure out what to do tomorrow," Tim answered.

"What if you fall asleep?" I asked.

"You can talk to me. We can sing. We'll make it."

For several hours we drove, talked, and sang hymns like "A Mighty Fortress," "Let the Lower Lights Be Burnin'," and "Safe in the Arms of Jesus." It made the time go by fast.

Finally we came to an all-night restaurant and fillin' station. It was the only one in town, and luckily for us, their gas was priced right—only seventeen cents a gallon. Gasoline had been less till President Hoover added an extra tax. It was only a penny, but Paw complained about it every time he got back in the car after fillin' up. He'd say, "Now that the government's in the gas business, you can count on the price goin' right through the sky."

Anyway, we parked a ways back from the lights and went first to the station. Tim, with me by his side, walked straight up to the attendant, handed him the car keys, and said, pointin' back toward the car, "'Scuse me, sir. Paw would like you to fill that old Buick over yonder and check the oil. When you're done, will you put it back where it's at now?"

Tim said it so much like Paw woulda said it that I had to look at Tim real close, wonderin' if this maybe was Paw reincarnated.

"Why did he park way over there?" the attendant asked, all puzzled like.

I turned and looked at Tim to also get the answer.

"You was busy when we came up," stated Tim.

That's when I turned and started for the restaurant. As I stepped to the door, I could hear the attendant ask, "Where is your paw?"

"In the restaurant," was Tim's reply.

Just as the station man looked into the café, he could see me takin' my seat at the counter next to a man somewhere in his fifties. So far our plan was workin' perfectly. Paw woulda been proud. When Tim came in, we ordered, but then the man I was sittin' next to got up and left. Quick as can be, we moved over to a booth out of sight of the station. As we moved, we saw the attendant was busy and possibly had forgotten us. We soon left and found a place to sleep to the side of a run-down barn on the edge of town.

Forcin' our troubles from our minds as much as possible, we read from the Bible, with the flashlight, the twenty-third psalm. Only tonight it meant more to us than it ever did before. 'Specially the fourth verse: "Yea, though I walk through the valley of the shadow of death, I will fear no evil: for thou art with me; thy rod and thy staff they comfort me."

Then, prayin', we was soon asleep, sittin' up in the front seat of the car.

In a good-sized town in Oklahoma, we took a chance, drivin' almost to the loop. We parked in a municipal parkin' lot and went into a secondhand store to buy a few things like kettles, a fryin' pan, and a coffee pot. The things weren't much good, but we figured with a lot of scrubbin', they would do. Then we bought ten pounds of potatoes, some beans, flour, coffee, lard, salt, and pepper. We wanted sugar but figured we could do without. We locked everythin' in the backseat of the car. Rather than sit in the car till dark, we walked back into town. What money we did have was over half gone now, and so far we hadn't made any time at all. Shucks, we weren't even half-way to Arizona yet. Walkin' around the loop, Tim said, "Sal, we just can't go on like this. We gotta come up with a better idea.

"Like what?" I asked

"Don't know as yet."

We went to a cheap café and got two coffees, each one costin' a nickel. Tim was quiet, thinkin' real hard, and then, over the coffee and right out of the sky, said, "Sal, I got it! And I think it's gonna work!"

Next thing I know we was in a drugstore, shoppin' with Tim's crazy idea in mind. After that, we found a small hotel on a side street where we could stay the night. It was one of those walk-up affairs, with the desk at the top of the stairs. We had to ring a small bell for service. My heart was beatin' so fast I could feel it in my throat. "Just be calm," Tim said quietly, "and don't say nothin'. I will handle this."

Just then, a curtain parted and the hotel clerk moved to the desk. He was mebby in his fifties, wearin' a mustache and his hair combed over clear from his right ear to his left ear, pretendin' he wasn't really bald. He put both of his hands on the desk and looked at us all suspicious like. "Can I help you?"

I held on to Tim's hand and held my breath, waitin' to hear what Tim was gonna say this time.

"Howdy. We're lookin' for a room."

The man adjusted his glasses and looked at us over the top of 'em. Then he smiled and said like he had us all figured. "And this must be your wife?"

Just as Tim was 'bout to speak, the man cut him right off. "Look, kids, I've been in this business too long—"

Tim wasted no time, cuttin' him off just the way he had cut off Tim. "Mister," Tim said no-nonsense like, "we've come a long way. This here's my wife, and we're lookin' for a room."

"Yer wife, huh?" the clerk said with a smirk on his face, still unbelievin'.

Shakin' his head like he was all disgusted, Tim opened the suitcase, reached in, grabbed the marriage license, and slapped it down hard on the counter under the clerk's face. Then he said, "Yes, sir, my wife! And here's the license to prove it."

The clerk leaned in and tried to read it, but Tim, quick as he put it there, grabbed it back and put it in the suitcase before the clerk could get a good look at it.

Tim and the clerk just stared at each other for what seemed like a dog's age, with Tim not budgin' an inch.

The clerk had no choice but to let us stay. He pushed the register in Tim's direction. "Go ahead," he said, pointin', "sign right there."

While Tim signed the register "Mr. and Mrs. Clark, Nashville, Tennessee," the clerk got us our key. "You'll be in room seventeen."

We paid for just one night. After the hotel and what we spent at the drugstore, we had only a couple o' bobs left. Tim laid down the pen and took up the key. "Thank you," he said to the clerk, then he took me by my hand and said, "Come along, Ollie darlin'."

We walked off, thinkin' we had fooled the man. But shortly we would learn otherwise.

Our room was small, clean, and neat, with one dresser,

one chair, a bed, and a small clothes closet. The wallpaper was pink and white, with flowers in vases stacked atop each other. The window looked out over Main Street.

'Bout half an hour later, while I was still in the bathroom gettin' ready to try out Tim's crazy idea, there was a loud knock on the hotel room door. It 'bout scared me to death. I opened the bathroom door just wide enough to poke my head out. Tim was sittin' on the bed. We just looked at each other all startled like for a long moment. Then came another knock, this one even louder.

I watched as the frightened look on Tim's face slowly vanished and was replaced with a look of fearlessness. Like Paw, he shoulda been a Hollywood movie actor. He got off the bed, moved to the dresser mirror, fooled with his hair for a tense moment, then put on his "older face" and went to the door.

When he opened it, two great big policemen, lookin' like giants, dressed in dark blue with hats, badges, and guns, was starin' down at poor little Tim.

I could hear one of the policemen say, "William Clark?"

Tim said, in the same manner as Paw woulda, "Yes sir, that's me."

"We'd like to ask you a few questions, if you don't mind."

"Did I do somethin' wrong?" Tim asked all innocent.

"We don't know yet," said the other policeman. "That's why we'd like to ask you a few questions."

And then the first policeman said somethin' that sent chills runnin' up and down my spine.

"We gotta report of two runaway kids from Illinois." He said, "A brother and sister 'bout your age."

And then the policeman said somethin' else that just 'bout scared the gajeebies out of me again. He said, "We'd like to speak with your wife, if you don't mind."

And then Tim said, again with all the confidence in the world, "Why, certainly." Then he called out to me, "Ollie, darlin', could you come here for a moment?"

What was Tim thinkin'? How could I go to the door? I would ruin everythin', and then they would take us away, and mebby Tim and me would never see each other again.

Then Tim called out to me again, only this time louder, "Ollie, darlin', please come here."

I had no choice. If I didn't go to the door, then the police would get real suspicious and likely come in after me. So I took in a deep breath, said a little prayer, braced myself best I could, and walked 'round the corner where Tim and the policemen was.

"Hi," I said, tryin' to act all natural.

I will never forget the look on their faces when they laid eyes on me. Tim's crazy idea worked like a charm. Under my dress I had padded my belly with the cotton battin' and tape we bought at the five and dime. It made me look like I was in the family way, expectin' with child.

Tim put his arm 'round my shoulders, pulled me in tight, and said with great pride, "This here's my wife, Ollie. Now what would you like to ask us?"

The policemen looked at each other with empty faces, then back down at us. "I'm afraid we've made a mistake here." The largest of the two then said, "Sorry to have bothered you. We hope you enjoy your stay."

Tim and me said our good-byes, closed the door, and just stared at each other for the longest time tryin' to figure out how they found out about us. Only thing we could figure was that Mr. Roberts found the blank Western Union telegram paper in the trash and figured we musta lied to him 'bout our uncle and aunt comin' from Oregon to get us. That was a mistake we would not make again. That night we slept better 'n ever. It was the first bed and bath we'd had since leavin' Illinois.

Nineteen

TRAIN TICKETS

SUNDAY MORNIN', WITH TIM'S HELP, WE PADDED AND TAPED me up again. When we was all through, I looked like I was mebby four months expectin'. We checked out of the hotel, had a coffee at a cheap restaurant, and then walked a couple of blocks to a nearby church.

We wanted everybody to see us, so we waited in the entrance hall till the singin' got started, then took off our coats and went in. The sight took my breath away. 'Twas a beautiful church, with a gloriously high ceilin' and tall, arched windows down both sides, lettin' in the sun. The church was chock-full of people, old and young alike, and they was all singin' loud and clear that beautiful and inspirin' hymn "How Great Thou Art." 'Twas one of Paw's very favorites. Tim carried the old suitcase in one hand, and I carried the worn-out Bible. Arm in arm, we joined in singin' right along with everybody else—

> *O Lord my God, when I in awesome wonder*
> *Consider all the worlds thy hands have made,*
> *I see the stars, I hear the rollin' thunder . . .*

As we was walkin' down the aisle, I dreamed I was

walkin' down the aisle in a pretty white dress to get married to Ben. There was Ben at the front of the church. He was so handsome standin' next to the minister, dressed fine and wearin' a big smile. Tim, as my nearest next of kin, was givin' me away. It lasted only a second or two and then it was gone.

It seemed like it was takin' us forever to get to the front of the church, with everybody's eyes on us and all. Finally we got to the very front and took our seat. Like I said, we wanted them to look, and I don't think any of them missed us. When we sat down, the man choristerin' the music gave us a nod and a kindly smile.

When the song came to its end, the minister stood and moved to the stand, placed both hands on it, gave a nice welcome, then began his preachin'. He was tall and skinny to the bone but had a voice that carried to the top of the high ceilin' and to the end of the church. He had everyone's attention. Only thing one could hear would be a baby in her mama's arms cryin' now and then. It was a good sermon, just not the one we were wantin' or expectin' to hear. It was 'bout liars and how the good book says that liars will have their part in the lake of burnin' fire.

My whole body was screamin' out. I was sufferin' so much with guilt I was beginnin' to feel sick inside. I turned to Tim and whispered, "I just can't do it. I can't tell all these people a big whopper."

"Neither can I," Tim whispered. "Soon as this is over, we'll get out fast."

As the last "amen" was said, we got up and headed for the door. 'Bout halfway down the aisle, a big fella stepped out of his seat in front of us and shook Tim's hand. "Strangers here?" he asked.

"Just passin' through," said Tim.

Right then the big fella's little girl, who was mebby three or four years old, began pokin' at my stomach causin' me to have frightful visions of cotton and tape droppin' from under my dress onto the church floor. Thank goodness her Maw stepped forward and pulled her little girl's hand away.

Several more crowded 'round us, askin' the same questions. Again Tim said we was just passin' through.

"When does your train leave?" asked someone.

"Can't afford no train," Tim answered. "Wish we could. We're hitchhikin'."

I could see some of them shakin' their heads when Tim said we was hitchhikin'.

How could we tell them the truth and say, "Brothers and sisters, we came in here to clip you for all we could, but after hearin' your minister preach 'bout lyin', we changed our minds."

All of a sudden, a peculiar thing started to happen. Several started shakin' hands all over again, with Tim. Only this time they was slippin' Tim a little foldin' green, tryin' to hide it as they did. Tim would shake with one hand, then would have to pass the foldin' green to the other hand before shakin' again. Several of them did the same thing with me.

The preacher pressed through the crowd and introduced hisself. We thanked him and told him how much we liked his preachin', and then he asked, "Where're you goin'?"

"Idaho," Tim answered, which was news to me.

The preacher then asked, "Where in Idaho?"

Like everyone else, I turned to Tim to hear what he

was gonna say. Without blinkin' an eye, Tim said, "Twin Falls. Goin' there to live with my uncle."

I knew right off why Tim said Twin Falls. 'Cause four years ago, we spent a month there harvestin' dry beans. Paw always said, "If you're gonna be makin' up a story, best you know somethin' 'bout what you're sayin', 'cause if you don't, it might could get you into a whole lotta trouble."

Well now, this preacher is no one's fool, I can tell you. Lookin' Tim in the eye after lookin' me over, he proclaimed, "You kids are all mighty young, aren't you?" We knew he was thinkin' we probably wasn't married. More folks were gatherin' around now, and I could feel my face gettin' hotter and brighter by the tick.

"Yes, sir," Tim said. "We're mighty young, but we're married legal, and we've got a license to prove it."

"Why doesn't your uncle send for you like he should?" the preacher inquired.

Lookin' that preacher right in the eyes, Tim said like what he was sayin' was the gospel truth, "It wouldn't be right to ask him for that kinda help. You see, my uncle has a house full o' kids with not much to spare, but he is willin' to help till I can find somethin'."

"My, you poor children," said a motherly lookin' woman steppin' into the circle. "And you, my poor child, in that condition."

A man who we saw sittin' on the stand with the preacher said, "Maybe we can fix it with the Salvation Army to send you on."

Now, we sure couldn't have none of that—just can't have them askin' questions and checkin' with an uncle we don't got. But heck, what was I frettin' about? Tim, I was certain, had all the answers already worked out in his head. And so he did. He looked up right in the preacher's face, never battin' an eye.

"Mister," said Tim, "we stopped travelin' long enough to worship like it's our habit, not to come here askin' for help. We try not to ask nobody for nothin' 'cept a ride now and then, and we ain't takin' charity from the Salvation Army, Red Cross, or what have you. With God's help, we'll make it okay."

Now, one and all were impressed one way or 'nother with Tim's speech, includin' myself. If I had a bob on me, I woulda gived it right over to Tim. That's how convincin' he was. Mosta them folks admired our spunk, and most all felt sorry for us. If'n they knew that just weeks ago we lost our dear wonderful Maw and Paw on the very same day, they'd really be feelin' sorry for us. But we couldn't tell nobody the truth 'cause like Paw said, they might split us, and there was no way we was gonna let that happen.

Just then, the motherly woman and her husband that had first spoken to us—a Mr. and Mrs. Kendall, as I recall—asked us to come to dinner. We was so weak from hunger that we couldn't say no even if we wanted to. Besides, it would save the money we already got from the church members for our trip. They invited us to stay all night, but that we refused. Like Tim told them, "Never can tell—might miss a good ride, and 'tis best we be a-gettin' and a-goin'.'"

Mrs. Kendall fixed a big pork roast with mashed potatoes, sauerkraut, and preserved applesauce. 'Twas the best dinner we'd had since leavin' Illinois.

Just as they was fixin' to take us to the highway, the phone rang. It was the minister callin'. Seems he and the deacons got together and bought us a ticket to Twin Falls, Idaho, on the 11:45 flyer. Neither of us, hard as we tried, could figure a way to get out of this one. I looked at Tim, and all's he could do was shrug his shoulders.

When we got to the station, the minister was there with some of the deacons to give us his blessin' and see that we got on our way. We collected a few more bobs, then boarded the train, sittin' close to the window, where we could see everyone on the platform. They all stood there, wavin' and smilin', till the train started rollin'.

Naturally the first time the train stopped, we got right off. Our concern was to get back to our car and get a-goin' to Arizona. We traded the rest of the ticket in for cash, Tim tellin' the depot agent that I just couldn't make the trip—thought I could but guessed we would wait till later.

Twenty

CAUGHT IN A BLIZZARD

DUE TO THE TRAIN SCHEDULES, WE COULDN'T GET BACK TO town till middle of the night. We walked 'bout three miles to get to our car, then drove out to the country to sleep. It wasn't hard to find a spot, as Oklahoma is nothin' but hills, gullies, and timber.

After sleepin' most of the day, we started west after dark, hopin' against hope that mebby we would find our friends somewhere in Arizona. With the money we got at the church and for the train ticket refund, we stopped and bought an extra wheel, spare tire, jack, and what tools we had to have. We also got more groceries and a five-gallon gas can. We parked around the block from a fillin' station and walked back and forth, fillin' our tank with the gas can. When Tim put the can in the trunk and got back in the car, he said just the way Paw used to, "Now that the government's in the gas business, prices is gonna go right through the sky."

Just outside of Clinton, Oklahoma, we stopped at a truck stop. It was 'bout two thirty in the mornin'. As we walked in, we overheard two truckers talkin'. The one said to the other. "What's all the excitement?"

"What excitement?" asked the other.

"Back west," said the first one, "'bout twenty miles or so."

"Don't know," said the other. "But I'm goin' that way."

"Then they'll be stoppin' you too," said the first one.

"How come?" asked the other.

"Don't know. But there's a roadblock out there. They're stoppin' everythin' on wheels. Even made me open the back so they could get a look and see. I asked the cop what they were lookin' for, but he just waved me on after lookin' in my cab."

"Could be they're lookin' for bootleg," the other one said.

I should mention here that even though the congress of the United States already done 'way with the outlawin' of drinkin' alcohol in '33, there was still states that held back from goin' 'long with the rest of the country. Oklahoma was one of them states. The police was always puttin' up roadblocks and tryin' to catch the bootleggers, or "rum runners," bringin' smuggled alcohol 'cross state lines.

After hearin' what the two truckers had been sayin', we filled our thermos bottle with coffee and got in the car.

"Dang it all," said Tim, gettin' behind the wheel. "We can't go thataway."

So we went straight east, then took the first gravel road that took us north, hopin' to soon find a road goin' back west toward Arizona. After a while, the road curved to the right, so we knew we was goin' east again. Then we came to a T, so again we started north. For nearly two days, we sometimes went north, sometimes west. Most of the time we were lost, as those roads weren't all marked on the map like they should be. Sometimes we would come to a dead end and have to go back again. We coulda saved ourselves a whole lot of trouble and time if we had just waited till mornin' when the roadblock woulda been gone. Doin' all that drivin', we got a flat tire, which Tim patched usin' Paw's patch kit in the glove box. To add to our worries, the car was startin' to get a knock in the motor.

Finally we went west of Wichita, intendin' to get on Highway 54 goin' back through part of Oklahoma, Texas, New Mexico, and up into Arizona.

The sky was cloudy, a gray sort of a cloud that had been hangin' 'round most all night. There was no stars or moon in the sky. The land was all level here. In the summer you can see wavin' wheat for miles and miles, with a few oil wells spotted here and there. But now everythin' was brown, spotted with a little snow, which was almost gone.

We shoulda slept, but in this country, everyone can see you for miles, and soon someone would come to see what was wrong. We had no choice but to keep on drivin'. As evenin' came on, the sky was still gray. The highway was straight as a ribbon for as far as we could see. When it got dark, we planned to pull over on a side road or even a field, where we could sleep. But just as dark was settlin' in, the wind started blastin' from the north. It was so cold we had to turn on the heater and put our coats on. Then, in the headlights, we saw the first flakes of snow—big flakes of snow the size of silver dollars. Harder and harder it came—a wet, clingin' snow that hung on the windshield till we had to use the wipers.

It was just our luck to get caught in that terrible blizzard of nineteen hundred and thirty-six. There are many who remember that terrible storm. It was said that in Montana the temperature dipped to minus forty-nine degrees. Later we learned that this blizzard would kill herds of cattle and wild animals. People were stranded clear from Montana and Wyomin' to down into the plain states. Schools and businesses were closed and snowdrifts as high as telephone wires blocked the roads and highways.

At first we didn't worry, 'cause we thought it would soon stop. But as the snow came faster and the wind got stronger, we started to change our minds. We could hardly see anythin' at all 'cept a white blanket. Seemed to me like the windshield wipers were sayin', "Gonna die, gonna die, gonna die."

"What's the wipers sayin' to you?" I asked Tim.

"No use, no use, no use," he answered, and I listened till I got the rhythm of the wipers—"no use, no use."

By then we knew this was goin' to be a real storm, one like we had never seen. We didn't know what to do. We couldn't park on the highway. Besides, Paw and Maw had told us stories of how people froze to death while stayin' in their cars durin' a blizzard.

Soon we couldn't see a side road even if we wanted to, because all was covered with a deep snow. We slowed to a crawl, not more than fifteen miles per hour. Even that was plenty fast, 'cause we could hardly see the highway no more. There were no other cars on the road 'cept us. Fact was, we hadn't seen a car for miles and miles. The only thing we could figure was that the radio had told people to stay at home.

Tim had never driven in a storm before. He stared ahead, grippin' the wheel all tense, and drove right down the middle as near as we could guess. Every once in a while, as needed, we stopped to get out and clean the windshield by hand. The snow was comin' down so hard and heavy that the windshield wipers couldn't keep up. The weather was freezin'. Just a few seconds out in it, we could tell it was below zero.

All of a sudden, we saw some lights ahead. "If that's a house," said Tim, "we're gonna stop." But soon our hearts dropped 'cause we could see it was just 'nother car comin' toward us. It was comin' as slowly as we was goin'. We just stopped till it went by, then we went on again.

Soon we saw a signpost. Tim got out, looked at it, then hurried back in again. He said, pointin', "There's a town of some kind down that way."

So we turned down that road. I don't know how we kept on goin' and keepin' from gettin' stuck. Can't to this day figure how we stayed on that highway at all. It sure wasn't 'cause we could see. All's I can figure is somebody was watchin' over us. Mebby even somebody was helpin' Tim at the wheel.

Again we saw lights ahead, and again Tim said, "If that's a house or anythin' at all, we gotta stop."

Sure 'nough, it was a house this time, sittin' not far from the road. The house was a typical ranch house, with a small porch with a railin' 'round it. At first we had a hard time findin' the driveway, but when we finally did, we took it around to the back of the house.

We jumped out of the car and ran. By the time we got to the porch, we was completely covered from head to toe with heavy, wet snow. We was just 'bout to knock when the porch light went on and the door opened. A pleasant-lookin' woman named Iva, short and a little on the heavy side, with an Irish brogue, exclaimed, "Gracious sakes alive, come in out of the storm!"

Soon as we stepped in, Iva called to her husband, "George, here's some strangers!"

Soon George came into the room in his stockin' feet. He was a little taller than Iva, but not much. He had a lined, pleasant face from which you could tell he'd had some hard times. Still, he was a happy Irishman, holdin' the hand of his granddaughter, a little girl about four years of age.

"Don't want to disturb you, sir," said Tim in Paw's drawl. "Just wonderin' if we could park in your yard overnight. Won't disturb you none, just sleep in the car."

Well, now they both looked at us and then at each other. Finally, the man said in his Irish brogue, "Now why do you want to do that?"

"Can't drive much farther," said Tim. "Storm's so bad we can't park on the highway. All we want to do is get off the highway. If we could have found a field, we would have parked there."

"And likely freeze," said Iva.

"Not at all," I said. "We got plenty of blankets."

"What you kids doin' out on a night like this?" asked George.

"Travelin'," said Tim.

"Best take off your wraps and come in by the fire, and we'll talk some," said George.

As I took off my coat, Iva said, "Oh, my gracious, and the shape you're in." Then she looked at George and said, "George, this poor child."

The house was big, with the signs of a clean housekeeper and the scent of fresh-baked cake faintly in the air. As we sat in chairs, the little girl started to walk past Tim. Pickin' her up, Tim asked, "What's your name?"

"Cynthia," she said.

"That's a purty name," Tim remarked. "What you good for?"

Lookin' up in his face, she thought for a second. Again Tim asked, "What you good for?"

"To eat candy," she said, and we all laughed.

Iva said, "My, look at that child make up to him. She's generally backward."

'Twas true. Tim had a way with all children. He could always make them laugh or cheer them when they was sad. There was somethin' in his smilin' blue eyes that they trusted right off. It warmed me inside watchin' Tim smilin' and laughin'. I hadn't seen him this happy since before Maw and Paw left us. I could see in his eyes that he was relieved and gratified that we was safe and warm from the wild storm that was gustin' and galin' outside.

"Now, what's this all about?" asked George.

"Just passin' through," said Tim. "Got caught in the storm. My name is William Clark, and this here's my wife Ollie. We're from Tennessee, and goin' to my uncle's in Arizona."

I could see Iva give George a doubtful look when Tim said I was his wife. Tim saw it too and said, "I know we're young to be married. I got a marriage license out in the car. I can go get it and show you, if you'd like."

"Don't you bother," said George.

"Have you had supper?" asked Iva.

"No, ma'am, we've been miles from nowhere since this started," said Tim.

While eatin', there was a million more questions and answers.

"Are you broke?" asked George.

"No, sir, we ain't broke," answered Tim, "not quite,

anyhow, but thought if there was any work hereabouts, I could make a little money—just to make sure we got enough."

After dinner, Iva and George took us upstairs to where they wanted us to sleep. Our room was a nice, big one, with one bed, which had a large feather mattress. We fell into a deep sleep listenin' to that wailin' wind in all its fury shakin' the house and rattlin' all the windows.

I dreamed of Ben that night. We was lying on the soft pine needles under the big tree. The birds was singin', and the silvery creek was runnin' by, and up through the trees I could see snow-covered Mount Hood climbin' into the sky. My head was on Ben's arm, and we was just talkin' and teasin' and laughin'. I woke from that beautiful dream 'bout six a.m., hearin' Iva and George stirrin' downstairs.

After washin', Tim went to help George milk and feed while I helped in the house. But Iva was like a banty hen, always worryin' 'bout me, insistin' that I take it easy.

The storm went on for two more days and finally blew itself out. The radio said snowplows were workin' at it, but many highways were still blocked and impassable. Thanks to the goodness of George and Iva, we were able to stay yet another day. Tim helped with the chores, but the best part of the day we sat around visitin'.

Another glorious night was spent in that feather bed. We planned on leavin' right after chores the next mornin'. To our surprise, George filled our car with gas and checked the oil.

Iva fixed us a lunch to take along. As we started to leave, Iva gave us their mailin' address and said, "Now, soon's you get settled, you write us, you hear? We wanta know how you made out."

Iva and George was some of the nicest people I have ever come to know. More than anythin' I wanted to leave a note tellin' them the truth about our folks dyin' and why we was lyin' 'bout bein' married and such. But how could I? So we just said our good-byes and got a-gettin' and a-goin'.

Twenty One

A CHANCE TO GIVE

WHEN GOIN' SOUTHWEST, THE CAR STILL HAD THAT ANNO-yin', agitatin' knock. Wasn't bad, but it was there, and we knew with time 'twas only gonna get worse.

Later, as we drove along, Tim said, "Be a good darlin' and get me one of those sandwiches Iva fixed for us."

When I opened the sack, there was an envelope right on the top. "Look," I said, holdin' it out for Tim to see.

"Open it," he said.

Inside was a short note and three five-dollar bills. The note read:

> *Dear children,*
>
> *We have a child of our own. If she was havin' the trouble you are havin', I would be prayin' for some-one to help out. Knowin' your pride, you wouldn't accept money without workin' for it. Please accept this small gift in the same spirit in which it is given. We only wanted to help what we could.*
>
> *Your friends,*
> *George and Iva*

After crossin' just the very corner of northwest Oklahoma, we knew of a good place to camp and cook 'cause we'd been there before. It had plenty of wood and water. As we drove up, we saw a car that was overloaded and a man and woman sittin' and starin' into a campfire. The woman was holdin' a little baby. They looked weary and weighed down with worry. As we came to a stop, Tim rolled down the window and said, "Howdy, stranger."

"Howdy. Come set a spell," said the man.

Then we saw a few serious-eyed, sober-faced young'uns comin' out of the bushes. Soon as I saw them, I knew they was migrants just like us. The man said, reachin' for a pot over the fire, "Here, have some coffee."

We joined them by the fire and drank the coffee. Soon as we tasted it, we knew, from experience, it was grounds cooked over and that these folks were havin' a hard go of it just like us.

"How 'bout we share your fire and our groceries?" Tim asked.

The man slowly looked up at Tim like Tim was some kind of angel come down from heaven with the answer to his prayer. He looked to his wife, who, we could see by the light of the fire, had tears fillin' up her eyes.

Lookin' back at us, the stranger said, "Can't take from you young'uns."

"Shucks, we got more than we need," I said.

Tellin' a whopper was a whole lot more fun when you're givin' somethin' away 'stead of when you're tryin' to git somethin'.

"Sure," said Tim, "been mighty lucky the last few days. Got more than we'll use."

Tim and I got out our groceries and brought them to

the fire. While the wife and I fixed a meal, Tim played with the young'uns.

We learned that they was plum broke and had been livin' for a week on only green onions that they'd gleaned from a farmer's field. They hadn't had one thing to eat that whole day and finally said a prayer for help just before we drove in.

What we cooked 'bout cleaned us out, but they didn't know that.

As we was eatin', their Paw said, "It just don't seem right takin' from you young'uns."

"We got plenty," Tim assured him again.

Later, as they was leavin', Tim slipped five bobs to the oldest child, who was mebby eight or nine years old, and told him to give it to his Paw after a while. Five bobs went a long way then. You could buy two eggs, bacon, toast, pie, and coffee for twenty-five cents.

Before we went to sleep, we read from our Bible and thanked God that we could help someone else for a change.

Twenty-Two

SEARCHING FOR FRIENDS

HOW THANKFUL WE WERE TO GET INTO ARIZONA! WE COULD take our coats off then, even roll the windows down, at least durin' the day. Oh, how badly we wanted to find the Musgroves or Sawyers. We knew we could come ever so close to them and not know it. But there was really no sure place to look. They might be in California or even in Florida, for all we knew, or just 'round the next corner. My greatest fear was to think that as we was pullin' outta someplace, Ben and his family might be pullin' in right behind us. But I guess chances of that happenin' was slim to none. 'Twas a big country, this United States of America, as we understood more than most, and chances of Ben and his family bein' anywhere 'round where we were was highly unlikely. Only one thing to do, and that was to trust in the good Lord and pray that the end of this journey would find me and Ben together again.

Still, the car was knockin', and it was gettin' worse. "We gotta get it fixed, or we might end up afoot," said Tim.

We parked just a short way from a garage early one mornin' and walked in.

"Mister," said Tim to the mechanic, "Paw would like

for you to get his car fixed. He had to go to work."

"What's wrong with it?" asked the mechanic.

"The main is knockin'. Whatever it is, Paw says to fix it."

Later we watched from 'cross the street and saw him drive our car in. We walked away with our suitcase, not knowin' how we was gonna gather up 'nough money to get our car back.

We started walkin' down a gravel road from Mesa in the general direction toward Phoenix. Though it was a hot day, we still took our coats, as the nights were chilly. We stopped at every farmhouse and talked with every rancher about work. But all in all, they said Tim was too young. They was always askin' the same questions: What are you children doin'? Where are you goin'? And why? Our story changed some but was 'bout always the same: We're goin' to Tim's uncle's to live. Yes, we're married. No, he can't send money for us to go on, but once we got to him, he would give Tim a job feedin' cattle.

Several people offered us a ride, but we turned them down so's we could walk from house to house. At each house, we asked if anyone knew the Musgroves or the Sawyers. The answer was always no. Many asked us in, and we would eat. Some of them would give us a dollar or two; a few gave us five.

The first night out, we stayed on the side roads so's we would miss the police. After dark, it started rainin' like the dickens. Luckily we came upon a used car lot, sneaked in, and found a car that was unlocked. We climbed in and slept till early dawn, me in the back and Tim in the front. The next night found us inside a large culvert pipe runnin' under the highway.

For days we walked and walked, tryin' to find work so we could get the car back. Durin' that time, some lady felt sorry for us and gave us a suitcase full of baby clothes. Later we gave them to a migrant woman who was more than happy to get them. Another night we slept in a haystack. Another time in a boxcar. When Sunday arrived, we went to a church and came out a few bobs richer.

Monday we went back to the garage. Yes, the car was fixed. It cost a little over thirty dollars to get it back. After payin' that, we didn't have much left. We told the mechanic Paw would get it late that night and asked him to park it outside and give us the keys, which he did. Then Tim came up with another great idea. After dark, we picked up the car, drove to another used car lot, pulled in next to the other cars, and slept till dawn. Next day we kept lookin' and hopin' to find someone we knew.

Twenty-Three

THE IMPERIAL VALLEY

WE HUNG AROUND THE PHOENIX AREA FOR ANOTHER WEEK, but still no sign of our friends. We figured it was time to be a-gettin' and a-goin'. We decided to try our luck in California's Imperial Valley. We got on the Interstate 8 and headed west two hundred and forty miles. Paw always said instead of callin' it the Imperial Valley they shoulda called it the "Valley of the Sun," 'cause the sun shined more there than any other place in the whole United States. "'Tis a fact," Paw would always say.

Me and Tim and our folks had been comin' there for 'most six years—mostly to harvest sugar beets and carrots. 'Twas backbreakin' work harvestin' them beets. As hard as pickin' fruit all day from a ladder was, I woulda much sooner done that than beet harvestin'. Tim and me would be bendin' over mebby eight, ten hours a day, yankin' and pullin' them stubborn roots up outta the dry ground by their leaves and bangin' them together to knock off the loose dirt.

Lookin' down them acres and acres of rows seemed like they was never endin'. Pull with all our might, then knock them beets together. Pull again, then knock 'em together. After'n a couple of days of doin' that kinda work, I'd be dreamin' about it in my sleep. Maw and Paw would follow us with beet hooks, which was somethin' between a billhook and a sickle, whackin' off the beets' crowns and leaves and then layin' the beets in rows for the carts to come by. Other young'uns would jump out of them carts and toss in the beets. After the beets was picked, they was grinded up and had the juice squeezed outta them. Then they was boiled down to make sugar. The part that was ground up and left over after the sugar was made was the syrup. Durin' those scarce times when hay costs was too dear, farmers would take this syrup and mix it with straw to feed their cattle so as to fatten them up for market.

Best thing 'bout the Imperial Valley, far as I was concerned, was where it was located. It was way down at the bottom of California, right on the Mexico border, and after spendin' a cold, harsh winter workin' a farm in mebby Iowa or Kansas, the warm weather was a welcomin' pleasure. Course, in the summer the valley was no place you'd wanna be 'cause the desert sun beat down with no pity, with temperatures sometimes soarin' to a hundred and twenty degrees. But we were grateful that sugar beets was a winter crop. Least, that's what they were called in California. They was planted in the fall and harvested in the spring when the weather was pleasant both day and night.

When we got to El Centro, it was toward the end of the beet harvestin' season. We parked the Buick where we hoped it would be safe, then set off on foot to find our friends.

On our second day out, we met up with a family we had known in Florida 'bout three years earlier while pickin' citrus. Turner was their name. That night, settin' by their campfire, we were so depressed we just had to talk to someone. They were the first we trusted with our story. They woulda liked to have helped us, but really there wasn't much they could do other than give us some food and let us use some of their blankets to sleep with. As we talked 'round the fire, we learnt that they had seen the Musgroves in Florida. Mr. Turner was told by Ben's paw that after'n they left Florida, they were headin' to Idaho's panhandle to train hops. It only made good sense that from there they would be goin' to Hood River, seein' it was gettin' to be that time.

That night, sleepin' under the stars, I couldn't stop thinkin' 'bout Ben and wonderin' like always if he was lookin' at the same sky and thinkin' 'bout me. And then my thoughts turned to Maw and Paw and wishin' they was here with us and goin' to Hood River to see me get married to Ben. The thought saddened me so that I cried myself to sleep.

The next day, we was up early and said our good-byes to the Turners. Mr. Turner slipped Tim five bobs, which I am sure he couldn't spare, but that was the way of the migrant—always goin' without for somebody else.

The news about the Musgroves seemed to make us a bit lighter on our feet. We was anxious to be a-gettin' and a-goin' to Hood River. When we reached town, we stopped by the postal service office and sent a card by mail like Paw always did to Mr. Johnson and told him we was on our way and to be sure and save us a shelter. We never told him the folks were gone.

We walked to the other end of El Centro, where we'd parked the car a few days before, but when we got there, the car was gone! At first we reckoned the police had towed it, but as we investigated the area where the car was parked, we saw some broken glass on the ground. We knew it was from our car 'cause it was close by an oil stain in the dirt from where the Buick was leakin' oil. Ever since Paw bought it, it leaked. Only thing we could figure was someone who knew what they was doin' broke into the car at night and jiggered the wires. We know'd it was no use tryin' to find it. 'Twas probably over the border by then. We felt so helpless. We couldn't go to the police—last ones we wanted to talk to. Tim and me just held each other for a long time and cried in each other's arms. 'Twasn't just losin' the car, it was losin' a part of our folks. The old Buick was our home and the memories that we shared with them.

Didn't take long 'fore Tim's sadness turned to fury. "Shoot, dad gum it all!" he shouted. "Why'd we have to spend thirty bobs and get that knock fixed?" Then Tim looked at me and said, "Gotta quit this cryin' and carryin' on. Maw and Paw wouldn't like it much. Gotta quit cryin' over spilt milk and be a-gettin' and a-goin'."

That was it. Tim just picked up the suitcase and started walkin' down the road toward the main highway. I had no choice but to wipe my tears and chase after him. Tim never complained 'bout losin' the car after'n that.

Twenty Four

OUR TRUCK

IT WAS ALMOST A THOUSAND MILES, GIVE OR TAKE A FEW, from El Centro to Hood River. First day and three rides later brought us to the city of San Diego. Our third ride was a kind, young couple. They fed us supper and let us sleep in their apartment, me on the sofa, Tim on the floor. So far the good Lord was watchin' out for us.

When we didn't get a ride, we walked. The weather was cooperatin', and the scenery along Highway 1, which ran along the great Pacific Ocean, was breathtakin' and beautiful.

On our third night, we slept in another culvert pipe not far away from the highway. A frightenin' thing occurred while we was in there. 'Bout midnight, just as we was settlin', a big ol' coyote came runnin' into the culvert with his dinner. Both Tim and me screamed to high heaven. The coyote 'bout had a heart attack too, turned, and hightailed it out of there lickety-split.

We got rides with all sorts of interestin' folks. Got a ride with a bunch of Indians drivin' a sheep truck. That's right, me and Tim were scrunched in the back right in the middle of all them dirty sheep. 'Nother time, we rode on a truckload of chicken feed. We slept under picnic tables, inside junk cars, and under overpasses, when we could find them.

Nearly three months had gone by since we left Illinois that dreadful night after Maw and Paw passed on to the great harvest in the sky. It was on a Monday when we finally crossed the Oregon border. I couldn't believe it. We began to feel like we was almost home. But then, just on the other side of Medford, it seemed we plum ran out of luck. To save our souls, we could not get a ride no matter what. After'n about an hour of cars blowin' on by, Tim said, "I got an idea. C'mon."

I always loved it when Tim got ideas, 'cause more than not, they worked.

He grabbed me by the arm and led me down into the drainage ditch off the highway, where no one could see.

"Take off your dress."

"What for?" I protested.

"Do you wanna get to Hood River or not?"

"Course I do. You know that."

"Then listen to me and take off your dress."

As I was disrobin' there in the drainage ditch, Tim opened up the suitcase, where we had more tape and cotton. Together we began buildin' a new and bigger me. By the time we was finished, I looked like I shoulda had my baby a week ago last Tuesday.

Up on the highway, Tim told me to stand side-a-ways so as the oncomin' traffic would have the best and most advantageous view of my condition. To keep the tape and cotton from fallin', I held it up with both hands, which, accordin' to Tim, enhanced the purpose.

One car, then two, flew by us like we wasn't there,

then a third car passed but then miraculous like screeched to a stop, reversed itself, and backed up real fast.

"Get in," said the driver.

We got in the back, and off we went. Tim's idea had worked!

And it kept right on a-workin'! Never more than fifteen or so minutes would go by before someone picked us up. All up Oregon, Tim was havin' the time of his life makin' up stories. Course, everyone that gave us a ride gave us a ride 'cause they felt sorry for us—'specially me—and naturally they had a boatload of questions.

Tim told everyone that I was only four months pregnant. Well, normally lookin' much further 'long than four months, the subject of multiple births—mainly twins—kept comin' up. Everyone was certain I was havin' twins, 'cause everyone we talked to had a sister, brother, friend, cousin, friend of a friend who'd had twins. I got plenty tired of hearin' stories about twins.

Just on the other side of Salem, this old couple, most likely in their late seventies, drivin' a 1933 Buick was kind enough to pick us up. The car reminded us a lot of ours that was stolen, only this one was a lot newer and in a lot better condition. The elderly gentleman drivin' told Tim he had bought it brand spankin' new in Portland for a whoppin' eight hundred and twenty-five dollars. First thought I had was Ben and I could never afford somethin' so steep. But 'twouldn't matter. We could get somethin' for much less that would oblige our needs. Just thinkin' 'bout Ben started my heart a-racin'. Oh! I couldn't wait to see him again!

"Sure appreciate the ride," said Tim.

Lookin' at us in the rearview mirror, the elderly

gentleman said, "We're only goin' as far as Odell. Hope that'll be all right."

I looked at Tim and rolled my eyes in disappointment. We was so close. I almost asked if they could take us on to Hood River, but 'twouldn't be right.

"Odell's just fine," answered Tim.

The man's wife turned in her seat and said to me, "When are you expectin', sweetheart?"

"Any day now," I said.

She then turned to her husband all knowin' like and said, "Told ya."

As we drove along, enjoyin' the scenery out the windows, Tim asked, "How's the cherry pickin' been this year?"

And then the elderly man said somethin' that, if I was really goin' to have a baby, would have sent me into labor right there and then.

"Not so good," he said. "Late frost killed 'bout half the crop. Farmers got hurt real bad."

I could feel my heart skip a beat when he said what he said. Hopeless, I turned to Tim and said, "Tim, I'm not gonna make it!"

I could see the couple look at each other all panicked like. The elderly man looked into the rearview mirror, then buried his accelerator pedal clean down to the floor. Seemed like in no time we flew right by Odell and the ten miles beyond to the Hood River Memorial hospital.

When we got to the hospital, we all decided that I was havin' nothin' more than false labor, so we didn't go in. Since we was now so close to where we was goin', the old couple dropped us off at the dirt road that wound its way to the Hood River shelters. We got out of the car, said our good-byes and thank-yous, then took off runnin' down the dirt road. Wish to this day I coulda seen the look on the old couple's faces as they saw me holdin' fast to my big ball of tape and cotton and barrelin' down that dirt road!

We was so excited. All the trouble gettin' to Hood River was forgotten. All our troubles and cares was now behind us. Sure, we'd have troubles ahead but nothin' like what we experienced gettin' here. Tim and me was laughin' so hard it was makin' it hard to run. I was so excited and runnin' so fast that even with the tape and cotton on my belly, Tim was havin' a hard time keepin' up with my long legs.

I had it all figured. Had it figured for months. I would find where Ben was pickin', then ever so quiet, climb up his ladder and give him a big kiss. Oh, how he would be surprised. I could not wait to see the look on his face.

And then as we turned the corner, our hearts began to sink. The grass field where the migrants always parked their cars was all completely empty. There wasn't a car in sight. We came to a stop and just stood there catchin' our breath and just lookin' and starin'. Then slowly we walked to the shelters, which only deepened the terrible lonely and desperate feelin' that was smotherin' us. Like the parkin' field, the shelters were all vacant and deserted. I leaned against one of the shelters and started to cry.

"C'mon," said Tim, "Don't give up just yet. Let's go talk to the boss. Mebby he knows somethin' we don't." I prayed all the way to the boss's house that he would have good news for us.

The boss was happy to see us. He told us what we had already learnt, 'bout the late frost, and said he was sorry that we had to come all this way for nothin'. First thing we asked about was the Musgroves. He said they stayed over the whole week, even after all the rest had left, waitin' for us. Then he told us they had just left that very mornin'. When I heard this, I wanted to die.

"Did they say where they was goin'?" Tim asked.

Mr. Johnson just shook his head. He told us we was welcome to stay in the shelters long as we wanted.

"Say hello to your folks for me," he said.

We never told the boss 'bout Maw and Paw. He did pay them a real compliment. Said, just mebby, they was the best workers he had ever had.

We walked back toward the shelters, with neither one of us sayin' a word. Only those who've lost their folks and have no one or nowhere to turn to could understand the grief and sorrow we was feelin'. Back at the shelters, Tim went to sleep after a while, but I was so heartbroken, I got up and walked across the big field out to the pines and sat under that big old tree Ben and I used to sit under. I cried and cried just like I did the night Maw and Paw died. And then my grief and sorrow turned to anger. Forgive me for sayin' this, but I became angry with God. Why had He taken our folks? Me and Tim was too young not to have parents. And now comin' all this way and learnin' that we just missed seein' Ben and his family was more than I could bear. More than ever, I then knew how big this country was, and tryin' to find Ben and his family would take a miracle. But at that moment, I wasn't believin' in miracles no more. I had prayed every night for the past year that Ben and I would unite and be married right here under this big tree. What was the use of prayin', I thought, when nobody's even listenin'? What were me and Tim gonna do? We didn't have no car, no money, and no place to stay. Now that Ben was gone, I thought to myself, might as well turn ourselves in and be split up. That way, least we'd be cared for and have food and a place to stay. I was tired of back roads, hidin' from the police, sleepin' in car lots and culverts, and always tellin' whoppers. I was tired of the whole thing. The thought of it all started me cryin' all over again. And then, 'tween my sobbin's, I heard someone call my name. Figurin' it was Tim, I stood and looked back toward the shelters. What I saw lifted my spirits so high that I started cryin' all over again. Only this time I wasn't cryin' from sorrows, I was cryin' from happiness. It was Ben, and he was runnin' toward me! Only thing I could think of was that he had called the boss from a roadside telephone and learned that we was here.

Watchin' Ben runnin' through the tall grass, I can still remember thinkin', "Oh, dear God, please forgive me for not knowin' that You was there, that You was hearin' my prayers all along."

But then, just as Ben got to the pines and saw me, he quit smilin' and began backin' away.

"Ben, what's wrong?" I asked.

He didn't answer. He just turned and started walkin' away faster and faster and then started runnin'.

"Ben!" I shouted, loud as I could. "Where are you goin'? Come back!"

But Ben didn't pay me no never mind and kept right on a-runnin'.

And then, all at once, it struck me what the matter was. It was my stomach! I had been so used to wearin' all the cotton and tape that I forgot all about it. The hurt look in Ben's eyes was makin' sense now. He was thinkin' that I had been false-hearted and untrue to him.

"Ben!" I shouted and started runnin' after him. "Ben!"

I could see him gettin' into his truck. I was terrified. If I couldn't catch him, I would never see him again.

"Ben, it ain't what you're thinkin'!" I shouted.

Finally I reached the shelters, but Ben was pullin' onto the dirt road.

I was hysterical and cryin' out, "Ben! Stop! Stop!"

I was runnin' fast as I could, when all of a sudden I hit a rut in the road, stumbled, and fell face down. When I got back to my feet and began runnin' again, the tape and cotton began comin' apart and fallin' from under my dress, leavin' a trail behind me.

"Ben! Please! Come back!" I shouted through my tears.

Then, just as Ben was 'bout to make the bend and drive outta my life forever, the ol' truck, all at once, skidded to a stop. In his side mirror, Ben had seen the cotton and the tape fallin' from under my dress and trailin' behind me in the dirt. Ben flung the door wide open and jumped out. The dust settled, and I could see Ben walkin' toward me. When he got to me, he scooped me up in his strong arms and kissed me. 'Twas a kiss I will never forget. It seemed like a dream bein' in Hood River again with Ben.

Settin' me down, he cupped my face in his hands and asked, "What took you so long gettin' here?"

Before I could answer, he asked, "How do you like our truck?

"*Our* truck?" I said, confused.

"Yeah, *our* truck. We're gettin' married, ain't we?"

Then Ben, with his twinklin' brown eyes, took me into his arms and kissed me again. "I love you," he said.

"Oh, Ben! I love you too," I said.

We hurried to the shelter and woke Tim. At first Tim

thought he was dreamin' when he saw me and Ben standin' there lookin' down at him. After'n that, we all three drove to Mr. Johnson's so Ben could telephone his folks to tell 'em we was here. The Musgroves, Sawyers, and some other families was all together, plannin' on followin' each other to Tanasket, Washington, to pick apples. But soon as Ben told his folks 'bout Maw and Paw, everyone drove back to Mr. Johnson's.

Twenty Five

SIDE BY SIDE

OUR WEDDIN' WAS JUST THE WAY I DREAMED IT WOULD BE—
beneath the beautiful pines with the sounds of the silvery
creek runnin' behind and snow-covered Mount Hood
lookin' down on us. A justice of the peace from Hood
River came from town and married us right under the
big, friendly tree. Tim gave me away as my next of kin
and also acted as Ben's best man. All our friends was there.
The only thing missin' was Maw and Paw. I'd like to think
they was lookin' down, smilin' on our happiness.

As we stood in front of the justice of the peace, I
couldn't help thinkin' of what Paw had said the day he
pulled Ben outta the Columbia. "Mebby someday you can
do somethin' for me." At the time, I thought Paw was
just talkin' to talk, but lookin' back, I know now that he
musta known somethin' none of us did. I never missed my
Paw more than I did at that moment.

When the justice of the peace proclaimed us "man
and wife," Ben reached into his shirt pocket, took out
two cherries, both sharin' one stem, looped them over my
left ear, then kissed me. Ben's folks and all our friends
started cheerin' and clappin' their hands. (We agreed that

a weddin' ring would have to wait 'cause Ben, with help from his folks, spent a whole lot on our truck.)

After the weddin', we had a lovely supper. Mr. Johnson brought tables and chairs from his place for the grown-ups to sit at while the young'uns sat on apple boxes.

A big cake sat on the middle table, with a tiny bride and groom settin' on top. Fifteen in all was there, not countin' the young'uns. 'Twas a joyous occasion.

Sittin' and visitin' with our friends, I could see Tim wander off all by hisself, down to the creek. As I watched him, my heart went out to him. If it wasn't for him keepin' the promise he made Paw of carin' and watchin' out for me like he did, I never woulda had the happiness I was feelin' inside right then. Excusin' myself from the rest, I wandered to where Tim was.

"Hi," I said, sittin' down next to him. "Whatcha thinkin'?"

He seemed all solemn and serious, never takin' his eyes from the movin' water. "Oh, just wonderin' where I'm gonna be a-gettin' and a-goin' now that you and Ben is married." And then he looked at me and said, "Whataya think, Sal? Think mebby the Musgroves would let me go with them? Could you put in a good word for me, Sal? You know, tell 'em I'm a good worker. Tell 'em I could help with expenses. Tell 'em I wouldn't be any trouble to 'em."

As he was talkin', an achin' lump came into my throat, and my eyes filled to the brim with burnin' tears and spilt onto my cheeks. I could hardly stand it. My little fifteen-year-old brother, tryin' to act all grown-up and brave like, was thinkin' he was all alone in the world now, with no place to go. Thinkin' 'bout the uncertainty, loneliness, and fear that must be tormentin' him inside right then stirred my insides up real good. I began sobbin' and said, "You are not goin' with the Musgroves! Do you hear? You are comin' with me and Ben!"

Tim looked at me with a thousand questions in his eyes. "Are you sure, Sal? 'Cause if you ain't sure, I can figure somethin' out. And what 'bout Ben? You two are gonna need your time."

With that, I threw my arms around him and began sobbin' even more. "Course I'm sure! I couldn't bear leavin' you behind! Ben already told me first off he wanted you to come with us. 'Sides, if you didn't come, who'd make the coffee?"

Tim laughed at that.

Then I said, "I love you!"

"I love you too, Sal!

As we cried and held each other, I could feel his tense little body slowly unwindin'.

The next mornin', we got up early and packed. Ben wanted his folks to follow, but they only shook their heads and said, "Best you young'uns go by yourselves and stand on your own two feet."

We gathered 'round, and Ben's paw offered a prayer of protection and safety for all. Then we cried, said our good-byes, and promised to return to Hood River the next year.

Ben, me, and Tim got in our truck and drove off, wavin' at Ben's folks and our friends till we was outta sight. We was headin' for Florida to pick citrus. As we drove onto the highway, I must confess I was scared. My thoughts went to Maw and Paw, wishin' in many ways that they was in the front seat, and us three in the back. As we drove on down the highway, Tim started to sing:

Oh, we ain't got a barrel o' money
mebby we're ragged and funny
but we travel along,
singin' a song,
side by side.

Ben and me joined in. Singin' like that slowly lifted my spirits and calmed my fears. I leaned my head on Ben's shoulder, and we continued to sing.

Don't know what's comin' tomorrow
mebby it's trouble or sorrow
but we'll travel the road
sharin' our load
side by side.

About the Author

ERIC HENDERSHOT LIVES IN ST. GEORGE, UTAH. HE IS A writer/director and sometimes producer of direct-to-video, family-friendly feature films and a few documentaries.

For almost three decades, Eric has been writing, directing, and producing movies for video release and television. While Eric found success with a 1978 theatrical release of *Takedown*, his specialty and success has been focused on creating family-friendly movies to the direct-to-video and made-for-TV market. His films have been distributed worldwide and purchased domestically by networks including HBO, Disney, Showtime, ABC, BYUTV, Nickelodeon, Starz, VISN, and PAX. Eric currently has eleven films on Netflix. His films include *Takedown, On Our Own, Dream Machine, The Robin Hood Gang, A Kid Called Danger, Clubhouse Detectives,* The Clubhouse Detective Series, *Baby Bedlam, Message in a Cell Phone, Horse Crazy, Horse Crazy Too, Down and*

Derby, and *Boathouse Detectives*, His films have starred Lauren Holly (*Dumb and Dumber*), Greg Germann (*Ali McBeal*), Pat Morita (*Karate Kid*), Lorenzo Llamas (*Grease*), Joe Piscopo (*Saturday Night Live*), Julie Hagerty (*Airplane!* and *What about Bob?*), Corey Haim (*Lucas*), and Bobby Costanzo (*Friends*).

Eric also wrote, directed and produced the Real Heroes series, a set of full-length documentary videos featuring the stories of inspiring Latter-day Saint athletes. Examples are Tyler a Real Hero, narrated by Steve Young, former Forty Niner quarterback, Thurl: Forward with New Power (with Thurl Bailey and narrated by Paul James); McKay: Million Dollar Missionary (with McKay Christensen, narrated by Dale Murphy); Kim: Vertically Challenged (narrated by gold medal gymnast Keri Strugg).

Eric is currently in predevelopment stages on a feature film planned for a theatrical release in the fall of 2012.

0 26575 59957 2